Marrying for King's Millions

MAUREEN CHILD

MILLS & BOON®

Pure reading pleasure™

First published in Great Britain 2009
Large Print edition 2009
Harlequin Mills & Boon Limited,
Eton House, 18-24 Paradise Road,
Richmond, Surrey TW9 1SR

© Maureen Child 2008

ISBN: 978 0 263 20995 2

Set in Times Roman 17½ on 21 pt.
36-0309-42438

Printed and bound in Great Britain
by Antony Rowe Ltd, Chippenham, Wiltshire

MAUREEN CHILD

is a California native who loves to travel. Every chance they get, she and her husband are taking off on another research trip. An author of more than sixty books, Maureen loves a happy ending and still swears that she has the best job in the world. She lives in Southern California with her husband, two children and a golden retriever with delusions of grandeur.

To the best plot group
in the known universe—
Susan Mallery, Christine Rimmer,
Teresa Southwick and Kate Carlisle.
Thank you all for sharing your
friendship, quick wit,
your brilliant ideas and your
never-ending well of patience.

One

"No way. Sorry, Travis, I just can't marry you." Julie O'Hara leaned against the closed door and kept her voice pitched loud enough so that it would carry to the man on the other side.

Clearly, he heard her.

"Oh, yes you can," he said, and even through the door, his voice was all steely determination. "Now cut the dramatics and open the damn door."

Julie's head dropped back against the door and she rolled her eyes to look at the high, beamed ceiling. Sunlight slanted in through the windows across the room and the golden wash from the sun created shadows on the walls that looked eerily like the bars on a cell.

Coincidence?

She didn't think so.

This was a huge mistake. She knew it down to her bones. The bad feeling that had been taking root inside her for the last month had suddenly blossomed into big, black flowers. Ooh, there was an image.

"Travis, think about this for a minute."

"Not really the time for any more thinking, Julie," he said. "The guests are here, the minister's waiting and we *are* getting married."

Her stomach did a slow pitch and roll and she clenched her teeth together and took a few deep breaths through her nose. Didn't really help. How in the heck had she gotten herself into this? Julie's eyes flew open when Travis King's knuckles rapped on the door again and she looked around the room with a frantic gaze, futilely searching for an escape route.

But there wasn't one and she knew it. She was trapped in this plush guest room in Travis's castlelike house on the King Vineyard. Just like the rest of the house, it was gorgeous, elegant and so far away from her ordinary world she felt like a servant girl who'd sneaked into the mistress's room to try on her clothes. Bad, bad feeling. And it was all her own fault.

She'd walked into this stupid situation with her eyes wide open. "Idiot."

"Open the door, Julie…."

"It's bad luck to see the bride before the wedding," she said.

"Uh-huh. Don't think that matters so much in our case, so open up."

Our case.

Of course their case was special. Because this wasn't your ordinary, everyday wedding.

It had all seemed so simple a month ago, she thought and instantly remembered just how she'd gotten to this place in her life.

"I need a wife," Travis had said. "You need a future. It's perfect."

Julie had looked at him, sitting across from her in a red vinyl booth at Terri's Diner in the heart of downtown Birkfield, California. In a small town, the diner was the one place where everyone eventually showed up. Julie had practically grown up sliding across the red vinyl seats.

Her first date had brought her here. She'd nursed her first broken heart over four double-chocolate shakes. And now she was getting a marriage proposal here.

Shouldn't there be a plaque?

"It's not perfect," she argued, thinking that at least one of them had to be logical here.

Travis had always been more impulsive than she—well, except for that one time when she'd married a man she thought loved her, only to find out too late that he hadn't. See where impulsiveness had gotten her?

Firmly, she said, "There's an easier solution, Travis. Just go find another distributor for your wines."

He shook his head, dark brown hair flopping across his forehead in a way that made her want to reach across the table and smooth it back for him. She resisted.

"Can't. Thomas Henry is the best and you know I never settle for less than the best."

True, he never had. Travis had grown up as a member of one of the wealthiest, most powerful families in the state. He'd long ago grown accustomed to being on top. Being number one. And there was nothing Travis cared for more than King Vineyards. Ever since taking it over from his late father, he'd put in the time and effort required to make King wines known all over California.

Now he'd set his sights on not only distribution countrywide, but also eventually international exports, as well. Apparently, Thomas Henry was key to Travis's plan for world domination.

"Okay, but you don't have to marry me to get him."

"No." He sat back in the booth seat with a disgusted scowl on his face. "I don't. I could marry one of Henry's hideous daughters instead. I told you, Julie. The guy's kind of eccentric. He's a self-made millionaire and now his big goal in life is to get his girls married. I'm single. Rich. Therefore, I'm prime husband material."

She smiled. "He can't force you to marry one of his daughters. This isn't the Middle Ages."

"I wouldn't put it past him to try." Travis smiled wryly. "But if I turn down his 'darlings,' he can—and will—refuse to handle my wines. I can't risk that. King Vineyards is poised for the next big step. Getting the distribution deal with Henry would put me on the right path. All I need to make it all happen is a temporary wife. If I'm already married, he won't be tossing his daughters at my feet, will he?"

"Why me?"

He grinned…and Travis smiling was pretty spectacular. She'd had a crush on him when she was a kid. But then, Travis was gorgeous, charming and his smile had been known to melt a woman's resistance at fifty feet. Good thing Julie was immune. All it had taken was marrying a jerk and being dumped. Just because she could admire Travis's smile didn't mean she was going to turn into a puddle of mush at his feet.

"A couple of reasons," he was saying and Julie listened up. "First, because we know each other and I know you need this, too. Second, because I trust you to stick to our agreement and not try to bleed me for extra cash."

She knew he was wary of most women because King men attracted gold diggers in greater numbers than the gold rush had back in the day. "But if I marry you, what makes me different from any of those other women? I'll still be marrying you for your money."

"Yeah, but on my terms," he said with a smile.

Hmm. He might think that was funny, but she didn't see the humor. Julie watched women throw themselves at Travis for years. And all of them had had one eye on his exceptional behind and the other eye on his bank account. If she allowed him to pay her to marry him, wasn't she just another member of a very large, mercenary crowd?

Julie groaned inwardly and sucked at her chocolate shake. When tumultuous times struck, always have chocolate handy. A good rule of thumb for life's little miseries. She didn't like the idea of people thinking she was after his money.

"I don't want or need a husband," she pointed out, even though she distinctly felt herself losing the battle.

"Maybe not, but you do need the money to start that bakery you've always wanted."

True. God, she hated that he was right. She'd been working like a dog and saving every spare dime for years and still she was light years from having enough money put away to open her own bakery. She couldn't get a loan because she had no collateral, and if things stayed as they were, she'd be at retirement age before she could afford her dream shop.

But was that any reason to get married?

Hadn't she turned down Travis's offer of a loan before this? She'd known him her whole life. Her mom had been the cook on the King ranch until she'd married the gardener and hung up her apron when Julie was twelve. As kids, Julie and Travis had been friends. That had lasted until high school, when Julie'd first heard the laughter about the rich kid hanging out with the nobody. Their friendship had gradually cooled down, but they'd remained "friendly."

Now that they were grown, they weren't exactly close anymore, but the memory of that friendship was strong enough that Julie hadn't wanted to borrow money from him and muddy up their relationship.

Wasn't marrying him even worse?

"It's one year, Julie," Travis said, tapping his fingertips impatiently against the white Formica tabletop. "One year and I'll have the distribution deal I want and I give you financial backing in the bakery. Everybody wins."

"I don't know…." She still wasn't convinced. And it wasn't just the thought of marrying for money that had her hesitating, though heaven knew, it should have been enough. Nope, there was something else bothering her as well. "And when the marriage ends, that would leave me a two-time divorcée."

How tacky was that? God, thirty years old and a two-time loser? Oh, if she could step back in time a year or two, she'd avoid Jean Claude Doucette like the plague. Unfortunately, she couldn't do that and that French rat was going to remain a part of her past forever.

"Yeah, but that first marriage lasted what? Two weeks? It hardly counts," Travis argued. "Besides, who cares?"

"Me."

"Don't see why. So you made a mistake. Big deal. You wised up, got a divorce…"

Yeah, she thought, after Jean Claude dumped her and arranged for a quickie Mexican divorce.

"Put it behind you, move on," Travis finished. "Anyway, he was French."

Julie laughed.

"And, I offered to beat the crap out of him for you," Travis reminded her.

"I know." She really liked having Travis as a friend. Was she ready for that to change? "And I appreciate it."

"So then marry me already."

"What would your family say? Oh, God, what would my mother say?" she wondered aloud, knowing even as she asked it that he'd have a ready answer. "This is coming out of nowhere and—"

"Hell," Travis said on a laugh. "They'll understand. We tell my family and yours the truth of the situation, but no one else. And let's remember how Gina and Adam got married last year, huh? It's not like this idea has never been thought of before."

"Yes…." Travis's brother Adam had married his neighbour Gina for all the wrong reasons, but their marriage had turned into something wonderful. Now Gina was pregnant and Adam was walking around looking like the emperor of the world. "But Travis…"

"No one but our families know the whole truth, though," he insisted, leaning across the table to look directly into her eyes. "This has got to look real, Julie. To everybody. Thomas Henry needs to believe it. So we'll play the perfect married couple. We can do it. It's only a year."

A year. A year with Travis as her husband. Oh, God, she was weakening and she knew it. Visions of a bakery with her name over the door were dancing before her eyes. Then something else occurred to her.

"What about…"

"What?"

"You know." When he just stared at her, she blew out a breath. "Sex?"

"Oh." He frowned for a minute or two, then shook his head. "No problem. Married in name only. I swear. Trust me, I can resist you."

"Gee, thanks. Don't I feel special."

"Besides, it's only a year." He said it again as if trying to convince not only her, but also himself, that they could do this. "How hard could it be?"

She hadn't expected to get married again. Ever. Jean Claude ensured that she'd never trust any man that completely again. But this was different. It wasn't as if she was going into this marriage all starry-eyed, expecting love to last a lifetime. This was business, plain and simple. And if she was going to do it, why not marry a friend? A man who didn't expect anything from her? A man who was going to help her make her dreams come true at the end of one tiny, tiny, year.

"So what do you say?" he prompted.

"Okay," she'd said on a sigh. "Yes, I'll marry you."

"Idiot," Julie said again the memory fading. She was back in the guest room, wearing an ivory wedding dress and trying to find a way to successfully chicken out.

"Damn it, Julie," Travis implored from the other room and she heard the banked temper in his voice. "Open the damn door so we can talk about this."

She shot a look into the mirror behind her and then tossed the lacy edge of her veil over her shoulder. Steeling herself, she took a breath and flipped the dead bolt. Travis opened the door a second later and moved into the room, closing the door behind him.

He looked amazing, of course. The bridegroom of every woman's fantasy. He wore an elegantly tailored black suit with a crisp white shirt and a bold red tie. His dark brown hair was swept back from his face and his chocolate brown eyes were pinned on her. In an instant, he looked her up and down. "You look gorgeous."

"Thanks." She looked the part of a bride, even if she didn't feel like it. Her dark red hair was piled up on top of her head, with a few careless ringlets pulled free to lay against her neck. The lace-edged veil was elbow length and tickled her bare shoulders. Her floor-length gown flowed around her in a soft cloud of gossamer fabric. Strapless, the gown dipped low over her bosom and hugged her narrow waist. She knew she looked good— she only wished she felt as good as she looked.

"I don't think I can do it, Travis," she admitted and laid the flat of her hand against a stomach that was spinning and churning with nerves.

"Oh, you're *going* to do it," Travis told her and took her shoulders in a hard grip. "We've got a garden full of guests out there and the musicians are tuning up. Reporters are standing out on the drive and security just caught a photographer sneaking in over the paddock fence."

"Oh, God…." He'd always been a favorite of the paparazzi. They followed him everywhere, taking pictures of Travis with whatever woman happened to be hanging on his arm. It just hadn't occurred to Julie that now *she'd* be a photographer's target. Her whole life was about to change and she wasn't sure she could go through with it.

"You're just nervous."

"Oh, boy, howdy," she said, nodding frantically.

He tipped her chin up, stared into her eyes and said, "You'll get over it."

"I don't think so," Julie said, willing her stomach to settle. "I've really got a bad feeling about this, Travis. It's all so much…more than I thought it would be. This is marriage, Travis. Even if it's only temporary, it's *marriage*. I can't do this again."

He frowned at her. "If you think you're backing out now, you're nuts. A King wedding is big news. A King being stood up at the altar is even bigger news and that's not going to happen."

"Fine," she said, snatching at his words desperately. "Then you dump me. I don't care. I'll explain that you've changed your mind and—"

"What's this all about?" he interrupted and stared down at her.

Julie refused to be swayed by the soft brown of his eyes. Instead, she steeled herself, stomped across the room and pointed out the window at the elegantly decorated garden below. There were two hundred people, sitting in rented white chairs on opposite sides of a white carpeted aisle.

A minister waited at the head of that aisle in a gazebo draped in brilliantly shaded roses and a quartet of violinists were off to one side, playing classical music for the waiting guests. Farther in the distance, a white tent, strewn with yet more roses, awaited the reception party.

"That, Travis," she said, swallowing hard

against the ball of nerves jostling the black flowers of death in the pit of her stomach. "That's what this is about. I can't face those people and *lie*. I'm a terrible liar. You know that. I get blotchy and start to giggle and then it gets *bad*."

"You're making too big a deal out of this." He strolled across the room, as if he had all the time in the world. "Think of it like a play. We're a couple of actors, saying our lines then celebrating with a party."

"A play. Great." She threw her hands high, then let them slap against the cool silk of her gown. "The last time I was in a play, I was a strawberry in the fourth grade pageant."

He sighed. "Julie…"

"No," she said, repeating herself now and not even caring anymore. "I can't. I'm really sorry, Travis."

"Oh, well, as long as you're *sorry*." His mouth tightened up and Julie frowned right back at him.

"I warned you that I was no good at this."

"You signed a contract," he reminded her.

Yes, she really had. He'd put their little agreement into writing and one of a fleet of King lawyers—or was that a herd?—had notarized her signature. So technically, she was stuck. Emotionally, she was still looking for a back door.

"This was a bad idea."

"So you said."

"It bears repeating."

"Maybe," he said and took her hand in his. "But it's the one we agreed on. So pick up your bouquet, we'll go downstairs and get this over with."

"I think I'm gonna be sick."

His eyebrows went straight up. "I believe that's the first time a woman has gotten nauseous at the thought of marrying me."

"First time for everything." Julie looked out the window again and her gaze seemed to arrow in straight on her mother and stepfather. Her mother was worried. Not hard to tell even from a distance, since she was wringing the handle of her new purse. Her stepfather looked uncomfortable, tugging at the collar and tie strangling him.

They didn't approve of what she was doing, Julie knew. But they were there for her. Supporting her. Her gaze slipped to the other side of the aisle where the King family took up the first two rows. There was Gina, pregnant and glowing, with Adam standing beside her, waiting to take his place as best man. Jackson, the youngest of the King brothers, was seated beside Gina and there were King cousins and aunts and uncles there as well.

Everyone was waiting on *her*.

But no pressure.

Beside her, Travis whispered, "Think of the future, Julie. Your future. In a year, you'll have your bakery, I'll have my distribution deal and everything will go back to normal."

She wished she could believe him. But that bad feeling inside wouldn't go away. And that, more than anything, warned her that "normal" might not be what either one of them were expecting.

Two

The ceremony was over fast and Travis was grateful. Hard enough standing there holding Julie's hand and feeling her nervous tremors rocking through her body. But as promised, when she said her vows, her voice had shaken and she got the giggles halfway through.

She really was a terrible liar, he thought, watching her dance with his younger brother, Jackson. But the deed was done now. He glanced down at the plain gold band on his left ring finger. Idly, he rubbed the ring with his thumb and tried not to feel like the small circle of gold was somehow a tiny noose shutting off his air supply.

This had been his idea after all, despite the fact that Travis had always avoided marriage. Generally, he stayed with a woman until she started getting that let's-get-married-and-make-rich-babies-so-I-can-get-a-fat-settlement look in her eye. Then he was off, moving on to someone new. It kept life interesting. Kept him footloose, which is just the way he liked it.

Now, he was married and looking at a sex-free year.

Hmm…

"Second thoughts?"

Travis turned his head to meet his brother Adam's curious gaze. In the last several months, there'd been a change in the oldest King brother. Oh, he still looked the same, but his attitude had shifted. He wasn't concentrating solely on the King ranch anymore. Now his life revolved around Gina and their coming baby.

"Not at all," Travis answered and thought that he was a much better liar than Julie. What did that say about him?

"She's a nice woman." Adam glanced out to the crowded dance floor where Jackson was spinning Julie around until she laughed out loud.

"Yeah, she is." Travis reached for his glass of merlot and took a long drink. "And she knew what she was getting in to, so don't start with me."

Adam lifted both hands and shrugged. "I didn't say a word."

"Yet."

He nodded. "Fine. I'm just saying that Julie's not like your other women. She doesn't have a heart of stone, so be careful."

One of Travis's eyebrows lifted into a high

arch. "I think this is where the old saying about the pot and the kettle comes into play."

Adam took a sip of champagne and let his gaze slide to the table where his six-months pregnant wife was sitting with her family. Then he looked back at Travis. "Exactly. When Gina and I got married, it was a straight-up business deal. Just like you and Julie."

"Big difference," Travis interrupted, not willing to hear a lecture or—God help him—advice. He didn't need any help here. He and Julie would do just fine. Their agreement was nothing like the one Adam and his wife had had. "Gina loved you. Always did, though God knows why."

"Very funny."

Travis shrugged. "It's different with Julie. We're friends. Hell, we're not even *good* friends. This is business for both of us. Nothing more."

"Uh-huh."

"Don't even go there," Travis warned, draining his wine and setting the glass down on the table behind him. "When the year's up, so's the marriage. End of story."

"We'll see."

Travis stared at his older brother and said, "What is up with you? Discover you love your wife and now you want the rest of us in your boat?" Grinning, he clapped one hand on Adam's shoulder and said, "Forget about it. I'm just not a one woman kind of guy, Adam. When Julie and I are finished, it's back to serial monogamy for me."

The song ended and almost before the last note drifted away, the band moved into another number. This one slow and dreamy. Music spilled from the stage, swept across the crowd and drew even more couples onto the floor.

Adam shook his head and said, "This is not going to be as easy as you think it will be, Travis. But I guess you'll find that out for yourself."

"Guess I will," Travis said, completely confident that *his* plan would work out just the way he intended.

"Now, I'm going to go dance with my wife," Adam told him. "Maybe you should do the same."

When his brother left and headed for Gina, Travis let that one word roll through his mind. *Wife*. He had a *wife*. Sounded as odd as the gold band on his ring finger felt. He turned his gaze to the dance floor and watched as a tall man with dark blond hair and a wispy moustache cut in on Jackson to dance with Julie.

Julie looked up at the blonde and her features froze in appalled shock. Something inside Travis jolted. He'd already started moving toward the couple when he saw Julie try to pull away even as the blonde leaned in closer to her, whispering something in her ear. Whatever he said had made quite the impression on Julie. She looked like a balloon, slowly deflating.

The crowd separating them seemed to get thicker as Travis moved faster. Instinct pushed him on. He slipped past people, pushed others out of his way and got to Julie's side just as she finally managed to shove herself out of the blond man's arms. She stared up at the guy as if he were a ghost and the blonde was enjoying her shock.

"Julie, you okay?" Travis came up beside her.

"Travis. Oh, God…." She covered her mouth with one hand and kept staring at the other man as if she couldn't really believe he was there.

And just who the hell was this guy? A reporter? A photographer who'd somehow made it past security? But where was his camera? Instinctively, Travis pushed Julie behind him as he faced the tall, lanky man who was looking at him with what could only be glee shining in his pale blue eyes.

"What's going on here?" Travis demanded, keeping his voice low enough that even the other dancers around them couldn't hear him over the music.

The blonde gave him a half bow and smirked. "I've only come to offer my congratulations on your wedding," he said, his English flavored with a very thick French accent.

Travis shot a look at Julie.

She swallowed hard and shook her head. "I didn't know. I swear I didn't know."

"Know what?" Travis said, turning back to the guy silently laughing at him. Something was going on here and he was damned sure he wasn't going to like it. Hands fisted at his side, he demanded, "Who the hell are you, anyway?"

"Ahh…" The guy held out his right hand and said softly, conspiratorially, "Allow me to introduce myself. I am Jean Claude

Doucette. And you must be the man who has just married my wife."

"I'm a bigamist," Julie muttered and the word tasted foul in her mouth. Well, this certainly put her "bad feeling" from earlier in perspective. Compared to now, that debilitating trepidation was like a day at Disneyland.

This was a nightmare. One she couldn't seem to wake up from. One where *both* of her husbands—dear God—were facing off like a couple of well-groomed pit bulls. Although, if she had to bet on who would be the winner of this weird contest, she'd put her money on Travis. The Frenchman who stood so calmly at ease had no idea just how much danger he was in.

"Yes, my dear," Jean Claude said, from his place beside the cold hearth. He looked suave and sure of himself, as always. His blond hair was swept back from his forehead. His pale blue eyes were locked on her and even from across the room, she read the humor in his gaze. He wore a well-tailored gray suit with a pale yellow shirt and a steel-gray tie. He looked relaxed, completely at home, as if he were enjoying himself immensely.

Julie had never hated another human being as much in her life.

Still watching her, Jean Claude leaned one elbow on the intricately carved wooden mantel. "You are indeed a bigamist. Such a shame, really. And so very…embarrassing, I think is the word. At least, it is potentially a very public embarrassment for your new husband."

It really was. The papers had been full of the wedding for the last month. Society columns were filled with speculation about the marriage of one of California's wealthiest bachelors. She could just imagine what would happen if they got wind of this news.

That distribution deal Travis was so concerned about would no doubt disappear and the humiliation would cling to him forever. Oh, God, she wanted the floor to open her up and swallow her whole.

Or better yet, swallow Jean Claude.

If her legs hadn't felt like overcooked spaghetti, she might have walked over to Jean Claude and slapped him. As it was, all she managed was a wince before she dropped into a wing-backed chair. The wide window beside her overlooked the front of the house. At least she didn't have to sit here and stare out at the wedding party.

They'd left the reception, where their friends and families were dancing and laughing, to come to Travis's study. Despite the room's size, its dark green walls, thick, colorful rugs and countless bookshelves gave the study a warm, almost comforting feel.

But it would take way more than the room's ambiance to comfort Julie at the moment. Her heart was galloping in her chest and her stomach kept twisting, as if a giant, unseen fist was squeezing it mercilessly. She shot a look at Travis and nearly groaned at the expression of pure fury on his face.

The three of them were caught together like survivors of a shipwreck. And two of the survivors looked as though they were each willing to throw the other out of the lifeboat.

Could this get any worse?

Oh, she really shouldn't have thought that question.

"I believe I saw some reporters stationed outside this…winery," Jean Claude mused aloud. "Perhaps I should go and have a quiet word with one or two of them."

Reporters.

Julie's head ached anew and the tumult in her stomach stepped up a notch.

"You won't be talking to any reporters," Travis muttered tightly.

"This is, as you Americans are so fond of saying, a free country, is it not?"

"Not where you're concerned," Travis told him, then added, "You start talking to reporters and my lawyers will be on you so fast, they'll take everything from you but that ridiculous accent."

Jean Claude's eyes narrowed, but as Julie watched him, all she could think was that he was so far outclassed in the whole really furious competition. Anger radiated off of Travis in heavy waves that seemed to swim through the room, making the air almost too thick to breathe.

"You are in no position to dictate terms to me," Jean Claude warned.

"Mister," Travis answered. "This is my house. I do what I damn well want and right now, I want to hear everything you've got to say. So start talking."

For a moment, it looked as though the smaller

man might argue, but then, he conceded and gave an indolent shrug, as if none of this was consequential at all.

"It is quite simple really," Jean Claude said in what Julie realized was a reedy, almost whiny voice. "The delightful Julie and I were never really divorced. So you have married a married woman, my good man."

Julie's heart stuttered a little, but she swallowed hard and pulled in a deep breath. She couldn't really believe this was happening, but it was hard to avoid the truth.

From a distance, the muted sounds of her wedding reception were nothing more than a soft, white noise. She glanced down at the gold, diamond-studded band on her left ring finger. Sunlight caught the channel-set stones and winked with a dazzling shine and glitter. Travis had only put it on her an hour ago. Why the devil hadn't Jean Claude stopped the wedding before it was too late? Groaning quietly, she buried her left hand in the folds of her wedding gown so that she wouldn't have to look at the ring again.

"I'm *not* your good man," Travis was saying and his voice was low, deep and threatening enough that if Jean Claude had had a brain in his head, he would have been backing up. Instead, he only picked up the glass of wine he'd poured for himself and sniffed in distaste.

"I am the injured party, *mon ami,*" he said, taking a mouthful of the cabernet and swallowing as if he'd had to force it down. The insult to King wines was unmistakable. "Surely you can see that?"

"What I see—" Travis said "—is a guy trying to work a shakedown."

"Shakedown?" Jean Claude walked around Travis, came to Julie's side and laid one long-fingered hand on her shoulder.

She flinched and ducked out from under his

touch. Jumping to her feet, she only swayed a little before locking her knees and lifting her chin. Damned if she'd let Jean Claude demoralize her again. Once in a lifetime was more than enough.

"I am only here because it is the right thing to do." He smiled, set the glass of wine down and looked around as if searching for something better.

"Oh, I'm sure that's the reason," Travis said and slanted a quick, hard look at Julie.

She met his gaze squarely and tried to tell him silently that she hadn't had a part in this. Whatever it was Jean Claude was up to, he was doing it on his own.

Smoothly, Jean Claude strolled around the room, inspecting the knickknacks, leaning in to check the signature on a painting of the vineyard, as if completely unconcerned about Travis's mounting anger. And, he probably was, Julie thought. The man was single-minded, she'd give him that. He saw only what he wanted to see.

"Why are you here, Jean Claude? Really." Julie asked the question because she wanted him gone. And the only way to accomplish that was to finish whatever he'd come to start.

"Why?" Jean Claude turned and gave her a smile most people reserved for a particularly bright three-year-old who'd managed to *not* spill his juice. "Surely that is clear, *chérie*."

She didn't bother to glance at Travis. She knew what he was feeling, because that anger of his was still vibrating into the room. Instead, she stared at the man she'd once promised to love and cherish, and she saw only a stranger. "Spell it out for me, Jean Claude."

He sighed. "Very well. You see, when I read about the wedding of my sweet Julie to one of the powerful King family, I knew it was only right for me to come."

"Uh-huh," Travis said, moving to stand

beside Julie, arms across his chest, long legs planted in a wide stance as if he were ready to do battle. "And the reason you waited until *after* the ceremony to speak up?"

Jean Claude gave him a pleased smile. "Why, speaking up beforehand might have alerted the press." He smiled. "Something I'm sure you would rather not chance."

The press. Julie could just imagine what the media would make of this. *Vineyard Tycoon Marries Bigamist.* Oh, wouldn't that be great? Or maybe *King's Queen a Counterfeit.* Her insides went cold and still. Jean Claude had come to blackmail Travis. It was the only explanation.

Travis sneered at him, raking the other man up and down with a scathing look that bounced off Jean Claude like bullets off of Superman. Clearly, Travis had come to the same conclusion Julie had. But when he turned that same sneer on *her,* she made a supreme effort to get past the disgust riddling her and find her own sense of fury.

"I had nothing to do with this," she told him, meeting his icy gaze. "Travis, you can't believe I would *help* him! You know what he did to me. How I felt—"

"Ah, *chérie,*" Jean Claude murmured. "There is no reason for you to explain yourself to him. And what was between us has nothing to do with this man. You are after all, *my* wife."

"Oh, good God." Julie shot her gaze at the blond man who had once captured her heart, and wondered what she had ever seen in him. Now she looked at him and saw him for what he was. An oily, sneaky, evil little troll.

A troll who looked totally pleased with himself.

"All right," Travis announced, his voice commanding attention in the otherwise still room. "Cut to the chase here, Pierre—"

"Jean Claude," he corrected.

"Whatever," Travis snapped. "What the hell do you want, exactly?"

Jean Claude smiled. "My demands are small," he said with a slight shrug. "I only wish my due as an abandoned husband…."

"Abandoned?" Julie's temper finally overcame her humiliation. She charged Jean Claude and would have slapped him silly if Travis hadn't reached her side in time to stop her. Still, even with his hand on her arm, holding her in place, she hissed at the other man. "You no good, lying snake in the grass. I didn't abandon you. You left me. Remember? You said you would get a divorce in Mexico. And then you wrote me a month later and told me it was done. That you were 'free of me.' Don't you stand there and—"

"Chérie," Jean Claude cooed, his pale eyes twinkling as if he were enjoying himself tremendously. "Clearly, you are overwrought."

"Over—" She hauled her right arm back and Travis gripped both of her arms before dragging her away from the other man.

"Did you ever get a copy of the divorce decree?" Travis whispered the question into her ear.

Julie shook her head, disgusted with herself as much as with Jean Claude. She'd been a complete idiot. Not only in marrying the worm, but also in trusting him to end the marriage, too. Her only excuse was that she'd been so hurt. So totally crushed, she hadn't really been thinking at all.

"No. He told me he would make me a copy but he never did." She shot daggers at the man standing there smirking at her.

"And you trusted him."

"Yes. Damn it."

Travis's grip on her arms loosened and when he set her aside, she could see there was still fire in his eyes. His mouth was set and a tic in his jaw let her know exactly how hard he was working to keep his temper under control. "We'll talk about this later," he said, then turned to face the other man again. "How much?"

"That's very crass."

"It's expedient," Travis argued. "Let's hear it. How much for you to keep quiet?"

Jean Claude nodded once. "Very well, be it as you wish. I believe—" he said calmly as he shot his cuffs "—that one hundred thousand dollars will convince me to not seek out the press."

"One hun—" Julie gaped at him, then turned to face Travis. "You can't seriously be thinking about paying him off. You can't do it, Travis. It's *blackmail*."

"I prefer to think of it as paying for privacy," Jean Claude mused.

"You stay out of this." Julie stabbed her index finger toward him.

"Julie," Travis said. "Let me handle this."

"No. You can't." She grabbed his forearm

and felt the corded muscles in his arm bunch beneath her hand. "Travis, he won't stop. This will just be the beginning."

Travis lifted her hand off his arm and Julie could only watch as he walked slowly across the room to his desk. Opening a drawer, he pulled out an oversized checkbook and glanced at the other man. "One hundred thousand. And if you go to the press anyway, I will bury you."

Jean Claude gave him a brilliant smile. "But what reason would I have to slay the golden goose, *mon ami?* No, your—pardon, *our*—secret will stay with me, I assure you."

Not looking at him again, Travis grabbed a pen, scrawled across the check, then ripped it free. He stalked across the room, folded the check in half and tucked it into the other man's breast pocket. Jean Claude lifted one hand to his suit pocket to pat the check, as if assuring himself it was there.

"Make no mistake, Pierre," Travis said, pushing his face into Jean Claude's until the other man pulled his head back and, at long last, looked worried. "Open your mouth and you'll regret it."

"But of course," the other man said and bowed elegantly. He stepped back, then crossed the room to the closed door. He opened it, then stopped and turned to look at Julie. "I'd forgotten, you know."

"Forgotten what?"

"Just what a lovely bride you make."

"Get out," she said, fighting the darkness that was rising up inside her like a toxic spill. The coldness swamped her, cutting off her air, spreading chills along her body until she was nearly quivering. "And don't come back."

He smiled again, then left, quietly closing the door behind him.

Seconds ticked past before Julie could force herself to look at Travis. She'd known him her whole life and yet, she had no idea what she would see on his face. When she finally faced him, though, his expression was blank. His familiar features no more than a hard mask, hiding whatever it was he was feeling from her.

And the cold rushing through her turned icy.

"Let's get back to the reception," he said.

"Are you serious?"

"Damn right I am," Travis told her, coming across the room to stand in front of her. "And you're going to smile and laugh and dance like you haven't got a care in the world. Understand?"

"I don't think I can. I'm so furious—"

"*You're* furious?" He laughed shortly but there was no humor in it. Just as there was no shine of amusement in his eyes or in the hard flat line of his mouth. "I just found out my new wife already has a husband. A black-mailer no less. And *you're* furious? Trust me when I say I've got you beat."

Yes, he probably did. Watching him, Julie felt his rage and understood what he must be feeling. But damn it, she'd been lied to, too! "I didn't know about this."

"I said we'll talk about it later." He took her upper arm in a firm grip and led her across the room to the door. "For now, we're going back to the party. We'll smile for the photographers. We'll dance and we'll eat wedding cake and we will not let anyone else even guess that there's something wrong. You understand?"

"I get it," she said, and was forced to agree with him. She so didn't need any more drama today. "More acting."

"Exactly."

"Fine." It wouldn't be easy, but with enough wine, all things were possible. "But then what?" she asked, looking up into dark brown eyes that looked as cold and empty as an abandoned well.

"When the party's over, we head to Mexico. To get you a damn divorce so we can get married again."

Three

Travis checked his wristwatch for the tenth time in as many minutes, then looked up at his brothers. Adam and Jackson stood side by side, looking so much alike they might have been twins. But then, Travis knew that all three of them were carbon copies of each other. With only a year separating each of them, they'd grown up close and had gotten even closer over the years. The King brothers were a unit. So much a unit in fact, that it was nearly impossible for one of them to hide something from the others.

For example, without even looking into their eyes, he was fully aware that they knew something was up.

"The vineyard manager, Darleen, should be able to keep things running around here while I'm gone," he said, glancing around the nearly empty garden area. The wedding and reception were over, the guests were long gone and now the catering crew was cleaning up. A veritable squad of workers was stacking the white chairs, dragging down the garlands of flowers, packing away crystal and china and whatever food was left over.

A low hum of anger still throbbed in Travis's gut. This should have been a good day. One to celebrate the fruition of his dreams for the winery. Instead, his dream was fast becoming a nightmare.

Shaking his head, he dragged his thoughts back to the business at hand and turned his gaze back to his brothers. "But if she needs help…"

"We'll be around," Jackson assured him. "Well," he corrected with a wry smile, "Adam will be. I've got a flight to Paris lined up."

Jackson ran the King-Jets operation for the family. Building luxury jets and leasing them to the wealthy of the world. They had plenty of trained, experienced pilots on the books, sure, but Jackson enjoyed taking some of the runs himself. Nothing he liked better than heading out to wherever the wind blew him. The job suited him. Jackson never had been one for staying in one place too long.

"And after Paris, it's Switzerland," Jackson continued. "Should be gone about three weeks, so Adam'll have to step in if Darleen needs anything."

"I'll be here," Adam agreed.

"Of course you will," Jackson said with a laugh. "According to Gina you're never more than five feet from her and you watch her like she's a hand grenade about to explode."

Adam scowled at the youngest of them. "Talk trash when the woman you love is pregnant. Then we'll see where we stand."

"Never gonna happen," Jackson assured him with a friendly slap on the back. Then he glanced at Travis. "Where did you say you and Julie were going on your honeymoon?"

"I didn't," Travis told him. "But we're taking one of the jets to Mexico."

"Mexico?" Adam silenced Jackson with a look. "Julie told Gina you were heading to Fiji."

"Changed our minds," Travis said with what he hoped was a careless shrug. He didn't want to get in to this with his brothers. There was no time for a long, drawn-out battle and no way would they have given him anything less. Travis checked his watch again, wondered what the hell was taking Julie so long to get changed.

"This have anything to do with the French guy who crashed the party?" Jackson's eyebrows lifted as he shoved both hands into his slacks pockets.

"Julie didn't look too happy to see him," Adam agreed. "I'm thinking he's her ex?"

"Damn it." Travis bit the curse off, low and hard. He'd hoped to just avoid all of this, since he'd rather *no one* knew about the blackmail. Especially his brothers. The Kings weren't the type to bow to extortion. And he wouldn't have gone along with it himself if he hadn't had to buy time, as well as Frenchy's silence. "Just had to be observant, didn't you?"

"Actually," Jackson mused, his features tight as he began to get the picture that something was off. "I wasn't paying attention. It was Nathan who cued me in."

"Great." So it wasn't only his immediate family that had their radar tuned in. Travis could only hope that the rest of their guests hadn't noticed anything odd.

The trouble was, there were too many damn Kings, Travis thought. His father had been one of four brothers and those brothers had spread out and created at least three sons apiece. Now they were all running different aspects of the King dynasty. Couldn't throw a rock in California without hitting at least one King cousin.

Nathan's company built personal computers and made them so well and so affordable, King PCs were threatening to take over the world. "What'd he say?"

"Nothing much," Jackson said and stepped out of the way as a catering crew member staggered past him carrying an oversized coffee urn. "Just that Julie looked like she was going to be sick and you looked like the top of your head was going to explode. Me—" he added with a sly grin "—I'm so used to seeing that expression on your face, it never registered."

"Thanks." Travis shook his head and ground his back teeth together. Nathan had noticed too much. "He tell this to anyone else?"

"Nope. Well, wait. Cousin Griffin and his twin Garret were there, too. So they know you were pissed. So what? You're always pissed about something, big brother."

He supposed that was true, but this was different and apparently, Adam sensed it. Jerking his head to the side, Travis's oldest brother shifted farther away from the rest of the cleanup crew. Adam didn't speak again until the three of them were standing in the shadows of the main house, surrounded by overgrown hydrangea bushes. "What's going on, Travis? Who was that guy? And what's he got to do with you and Julie?"

"He's an irritant." The hairs at the back of his neck bristled and Travis felt the urge to howl or hit something. His perfectly laid plans were threatening to crumble down around him. All because of one greedy bastard.

"Care to explain?" Jackson asked.

Travis glared at him. "Not really."

"Do it anyway," Adam said.

He blew out a breath and surrendered to the inevitable. "Name's Jean Claude Doucette."

Adam whistled. "So I was right. He's Julie's ex?"

"Well, that's tacky as all get out," Jackson muttered. "Why the hell did he come to the wedding?"

As the workers went on about their business, the muted sounds became nothing more than white noise. But Travis still kept his voice pitched low. "Because as it turns out, he's not as *ex* as we thought."

"Explain," Adam said.

He did. While Jackson and Adam threw astonished glances at each other and then him, Travis told his brothers exactly what had happened after the wedding. Watching their reactions, Travis felt his own anger begin to bubble fresh in the pit of his stomach.

"You *paid* the bastard?" Jackson demanded. "Are you nuts?"

"Had to," Travis said. "No choice."

"There's always a choice," Jackson told him, then paused and cocked his head. "You hear that? Sort of a low rumble?" When neither of his brothers said anything, Jackson said, "That's the sound of dad spinning in his grave."

Travis nodded. "Yeah, helpful. Thanks."

"You never pay a blackmailer, Travis," Adam said. "You should have called the police."

"Right. Because cops showing up to my wedding would look so great in the papers." Travis shook his head again and dearly wished he hadn't quit smoking two years ago. He'd only quit then to prove to himself he could do it. That his own will was stronger than the siren's call of nicotine. Well, fine. He'd proved his case. Now he wanted a damn cigarette.

"He'll only come back for more," Adam warned.

"Think I don't know that?" Travis shifted his gaze from his brothers to the remnants of the party. A tablecloth lifted lazily into the wind and a napkin skipped across the lawn, tossed by a breeze that rifled the leaves of the bushes where they stood. The sun was sliding down toward the horizon and painting the slivers of clouds in the sky a pearly sort of dark peach. And he was taking note of all of this in an attempt to not think about what his brain was chewing on.

Pointless.

Turning back to his oldest brother, he said, "I paid him because I wanted to buy myself some time. We're going to Mexico to arrange for a divorce and a quick—quiet—wedding. When we get back, I'll take care of the little creep."

"What do you want us to do?" Adam asked and Travis was suddenly grateful for his family. Sure, they argued and fought him and let him know when they didn't agree with him, but when it counted, they stepped up to help in any way they could.

"Keep an eye on him. Watch where he goes. Who he's with." Travis had been thinking about this for the last couple of hours. Even when he stood beside Julie to cut the cake. When he'd posed for pictures he didn't want. When he danced with her to thunderous applause. During all that time, he'd been planning his next move. He'd decided to hire a P.I., but this was better. His brothers would never betray him and the fewer outsiders who knew the truth, the better for him.

He checked his wristwatch again. Whether Julie was ready or not, it was time to go. "Look in to this French guy's past. I don't care how you do it but get me some information on him. I'm thinking this isn't the first time he's pulled this stunt."

"What?" Jackson almost laughed, then

sobered up again fast. "You think he marries women then goes around blackmailing 'em? Gotta be easier ways to make a living."

"I don't know about that, but I'm thinking blackmail's not new to him. He was really smooth. Wouldn't surprise me to find out it wasn't his first time."

"We'll do it," Adam said softly, shooting a look at the house behind them. "But what about Julie?"

Travis went cold and still. "What about her?"

"You don't think she was in on it, do you?"

"The million-dollar question," Travis said, turning so that he could look up to the window of the bedroom where he knew she was changing clothes, preparing to leave. "I don't know if she's a part of this. But I intend to find out."

"I don't like this a bit."

"I know, Mom," Julie said as she tried to

fluff hair that refused to be fluffed. She gave herself a quick once-over in the mirror and thought that despite everything that had happened that day, she looked pretty good. Her red hair was flat, but her sleeveless, dark green dress looked great. Frowning a little, she tried to tug up the bodice, but it fell back into place again, displaying a little too much cleavage for comfort.

Too late to change now, though. She was already behind schedule and if there was one thing Travis appreciated it was a tightly run ship.

"Why was Jean Claude here?" her mother asked from her seat on the edge of the queen-size bed.

Julie looked into the mirror at her mom's concerned features and for just a minute or two, she considered confessing all. But what would that serve? All she'd do was worry her mother. It wouldn't solve the problem.

Wouldn't make it go away. So, no point in opening this particular can of worms.

"To wish me luck," she said instead and forced a smile.

"Hmm…" Her mom wasn't buying it, but she wasn't arguing, either, so that was good.

"Look, Mom," Julie said, spinning around to face her. "I know you don't approve of my marrying Travis—"

"I have nothing against him," her mother interrupted sharply, getting to her feet and coming closer to Julie. "You know that. The King boys all have good hearts."

"See?" Julie argued. "It'll be fine."

Her mom wasn't finished, though. "I know the two of you were close when you were children, but people change and—"

"Mom, that was a long time ago." Julie's memories rose up in a rush, though. In seconds, she saw herself and Travis as kids, sneaking out to the barn to give the horses apples. Hiding from Jackson when he wanted to play with them. Following Adam around until he chased them off. They had been close. But that was childhood. This was now. "We're two consenting adults and we know what we're doing."

"But marrying a man you don't love and letting him *pay* you for it—"

"Wow, when you say it like that, it sounds really bad," Julie said.

"It is really bad, honey," her mother said and took both of Julie's hands in hers. "You've already had one miserable experience with marriage. I want more for you. I want you to love and be loved."

"Maybe one day that will happen," Julie said, sighing a little, since this wasn't the first time they'd had this conversation. "But this isn't about love. Travis needed a wife and I get my bakery. It's a simple business deal."

"Hmm..." Her mother's features twisted

into a disapproving frown and Julie knew that Mary O'Hara Hambleton would never be okay with this situation.

But it was a done deal now. Or was it? Since she was still married to Jean Claude, she wasn't married at all to Travis, so— Oh, she really didn't want to think about any of this anymore.

"Mom, I've got to run. Travis will be waiting."

Her mother swept her up in a hard, tight hug and kissed her soundly on the cheek. Cupping Julie's face in her palms, she said, "Don't get hurt again, Julie honey. I don't think I could bear it if I had to see your heart broken like it was before."

Julie didn't want to see that again, either. As miserable a creep as Jean Claude actually was, once upon a time, Julie had thought herself desperately in love with him. And when he'd tossed her aside, the bruises had been soul deep. She wasn't interested in ever going through an experience like that again.

Which is why this "marriage" to Travis would work so well. Neither of them were even pretending to be in love.

Julie hugged her mom, then stepped away and headed for the bedroom door. Her suitcases had already been loaded into the car, so all she had to carry was her slim, green leather clutch bag. Her high heels were soundless on the thick carpet and the cut-glass doorknob felt cold against her palm.

At the door, she turned to look at her mother and tried not to dwell on the worry in her eyes. "I won't be hurt, Mom. This isn't about love, remember? It's business."

Travis hardly spoke to her for the first hour of the flight to The Riviera, Maya, Mexico.

It shouldn't have surprised her any, but a part of Julie wished he would just say what he was thinking instead of sulking with a glass of scotch. Although, the fact that he was drinking expensive, single malt scotch, instead of his beloved wine, was an indicator that he wasn't looking to relax. He was looking to cloud his mind. So maybe she should be grateful for the quiet after all.

The flight attendant, who was wearing a crisp, navy blue skirt and short-sleeved white blouse, came through and offered Julie a drink. After a moment's hesitation, she ordered a margarita on the rocks. With the day they'd had, she deserved a little mind-numbing herself.

The attendant left a frothy pitcher of margaritas within easy reach of Julie, then disappeared into the cockpit to join the pilots, leaving the newlyweds alone. Great. Because being alone with a man who was so angry he wasn't speaking was sure to make the honeymoon trip a good one.

With a sip of her drink, Julie distracted herself by looking around the plane and eased back into the soft-as-butter, pale blue leather chair. The carpets were sky-blue, as well and there were two couches, as well as several wide chairs such as the one she'd claimed. At the back of the plane, there was a bedroom, complete with king-size bed, and a bathroom that made the one in her apartment look like a broom closet.

There was a plasma television screen affixed to the front wall, and a tiny kitchen tucked into a corner. There were a few paintings hung about and a vase, attached to a low table, boasted a stunning bouquet of fresh spring flowers.

It should have been ideal. Romantic. In any other circumstance.

But the quiet, broken only by the low, insistent roar of the engines, began nibbling at Julie's nerves and soon she was glancing at her new, would-be husband. Travis was stretched out in a chair closer to the front of the airplane. His long legs were crossed at the ankle and the only muscle he'd moved in an hour was his right arm, as he lifted his glass of scotch to his mouth.

She took another long gulp of her margarita and swallowed the Dutch courage before asking, "So are you permanently mute or is this just a temporary condition?"

Slowly, Travis swiveled his head to look at her then, almost lazily, he swung his chair around until he was facing her. His brown eyes were narrowed and the shadow of whiskers darkened his jaw. "What would you like to talk about?"

Good question. She didn't really even want to think about Jean Claude, let alone talk about him. But she knew that conversation was coming. No way to avoid it forever, but putting it off for a few hours didn't seem like a bad plan, either. She didn't want to talk about the money he'd paid Jean Claude, either, because that just infuriated her and she was fairly certain that Travis was still furious about it, too. Should they talk about how they weren't really married and that if that fact came out they'd both be publicly humiliated?

No thanks.

So what did that leave?

"Um, nice plane?" Lame, Julie thought. Seriously lame.

He snorted, shook his head and took a sip of his drink. "Thanks."

She wasn't willing to give up on this so soon. Now that she had him talking, she wanted to keep it that way. Julie had never been an "easy" flier. Normally, she was too busy praying frantically to keep the plane in the air to enjoy anything of the experience. Today, though, it was different. She hadn't bothered with prayer because she figured the day had been so bad already, karma wouldn't allow this plane to crash.

"I've never ridden a plane where I didn't

have the guy in front of me leaning back into my lap. This is much nicer."

He glanced around at their sumptuous surroundings and shrugged in dismissal. "I haven't flown commercial in so long I've forgotten what it's like."

Wow. More than a couple of words. They were closing in on an actual conversation. "You're not missing anything. Trust me on this."

Instantly, his gaze shifted back to her. "Well now, that's the thing, isn't it, Jules?" He was using the nickname he'd given her when they were kids, but there was nothing friendly in his gaze. "I don't know that I can. Trust you, that is."

Four

The ride to the hotel was a silent one. Travis kept his thoughts to himself, which was just as well, since they were black enough to form storm clouds inside the limousine.

Julie sat beside him, but they might as well have been in two separate cars. He felt her nerves like a living thing in the limo and he was feeling just cold enough himself to do nothing to dissuade them. She should be nervous, damn it. Hadn't been *his* fault they'd had to trek to Mexico to clear up her past before someone in the media found out.

He closed his eyes as that thought settled in tight. He could just imagine the field day the press would have blasting this little piece of news across the front pages of their rags. The King family name would be trashed and any hopes he had of moving his winery into the upper echelon of the business would have to be put on hold for years.

He simply wouldn't allow it.

He'd worked too hard, come too far for his plans to be disrupted by an oily Frenchman with a penchant for greed.

Slanting a look at the woman beside him, Travis watched her face as she stared out the window at the passing landscape. The streets of Cancún were nothing more than a colorful blur, shaded by the tinted windows as the limo sped through traffic.

But he didn't need to look at the scenery. He'd been here so many times, there was nothing new or interesting to catch his attention. Yet, Julie sat there like a kid at the circus, her gaze flitting over everything, despite her nearly palpable anxiety.

His last words to her repeated in his mind. *I don't know that I can trust you, do I?* He'd seen her face, the shocked hurt in her eyes, and still, he hadn't called those words back. It was just too neat that she had agreed to marry him so quickly only to have her soon-to-be ex-husband show up on their wedding day.

She had to have been in on it with the Frenchman.

The question was *why?*

With the agreement they'd made, she stood to make considerably more than a hundred thousand dollars at the end of their marriage. So why would she risk it all for a quick fix?

"It's beautiful here," she said now, and her voice shattered the silence.

"I guess." He didn't want to talk to her right

now, but he also was tired of thinking, so he supposed he was grateful for the reprieve.

She turned to look at him and exasperation glittered in her eyes. "Y'know, Travis," she said quietly, "I'm not the enemy."

"Well now, that's yet to be decided, isn't it?"

"Apparently." Julie sat back against the seat, crossed her truly great legs, shook her head and flashed him a glare. "I've never lied to you."

"So you say," he admitted with a nod even as his gaze locked on the slide of her legs.

"That's right, I do. We've known each other since we were kids, for crying out loud. Do you really think I'd *blackmail* you?"

"We used to know each other," he pointed out, still trying to look away from the legs she kept crossing and recrossing in an obvious show of nerves.

"What I can't figure out is why you're so willing to believe Jean Claude? You've never seen him before but you're willing to take his word over mine?"

"Why would he lie?"

"He's a blackmailer and you think lying is beneath him?"

"Why bother?"

"To make you *pay* him?" she asked.

"He didn't need to name you as a conspirator to get the cash. So why would he?" He watched her and saw a flash of fire in her eyes. So she wasn't all nerves. There was temper there, too.

"Because he's a creep and he wanted to do everything he could to make sure I was miserable and you were furious." She crossed her arms under her breasts and that movement was enough to pry his gaze from her legs. Her crossed arms plumped up his already excellent view of her cleavage. His gaze lingered for a long minute, until she was uncomfortable enough to ease her arms away.

"Seems like a lot of trouble for him to go to," Travis mused.

"Didn't take much on his part at all to turn you into an *über*-jerk," she said.

Now his own temper flashed and his was a hell of a lot more intimidating than hers. "Jerk? I think I've been pretty damn considerate, considering," he pointed out. "We're here, aren't we? Going to get you that divorce and get married again so that the deal still holds and nobody else is the wiser?"

"Yes," she said, turning her gaze from him to stare out at the passing sights. "And you've been a delightful companion so far, too, so thanks very much."

He fumed silently. She wanted him to be a companion now? Friendly banter? He'd had potential disaster tossed at his feet on his wedding day and she wanted good company? To hell with that.

Thankfully, their debate ended soon after

that. Travis sat up as the limousine approached the hotel. Castello de King, or King's Castle, was opulent, over-the-top luxurious and owned by family, so it would give him exactly the privacy he required.

It was a huge building, taking up half the block. The walls were a soft pink stone that seemed to shimmer in the late afternoon sun. There were round tower rooms on every corner and leaded glass panes of the windows winked with the sun's reflection. Built more than a hundred years ago by an American businessman who'd imagined himself royalty, the castle had been purchased by the King family several decades before and turned into a hotel.

But it was only in the last five years or so that the castle had been "discovered" by the famous and infamous.

Travis had always liked the place, and since his cousin Rico had taken over the castle, it had become one of Travis's favorite vacation spots.

Cameramen and tourists lined the front of the hotel, each of them trying to get a picture of someone interesting, and they all moved reluctantly out of the limo's way as the driver steered the car onto the property.

Travis imagined how Julie was seeing the place and took it in himself as if for the first time. The driveway was wide and circular, and swept past banks of tropical flowers in every imaginable color. A towering fountain stood in the center of the courtyard and water fell from its tip to dance in its base in an unceasing cascade. Doormen in full white livery waited to serve the wealthy guests who flocked here looking to be spoiled in secure, lavish comfort.

Travis could almost feel the lenses of the paparazzi stationed on the sidewalk in front of the hotel. Their cameras were no doubt focused in to help them in their quest for an embarrassing or incriminating photo of celebrity lives. But they were kept off hotel property by a fleet of security guards, who protected the guests privacy at all costs, which was only one of the reasons Castello de King was such a popular resort for the wealthy.

The limo pulled to a stop and before Travis could get out on his side, one of the doormen had opened Julie's door and offered her a hand. She stood, turning in place and admiring the view, as Travis got out of the limo to join her.

The look on her face was one of wonder—sort of what he imagined a child might look like at her first sight of Disneyland. And he was willing to bet that the paparazzi were getting quite a few great shots of the latest King bride. As long as no reporter thought to check into her background, they might be all right. God help them both if someone got nosy and discovered the truth.

"Señor King, it is good to have you with us

again." The older man had skin the color of milky coffee, snow-white hair and pale green eyes, crinkled at the corners.

Travis nodded. Over the last few years, Travis had become well known to the hotel staff. "Esteban, good to be back. Is my cousin here?"

Of course Rico was here, Travis told himself. His cousin rarely left the hotel that he'd single-handedly built into one of the most sought-after vacation sites in the world.

"*Sí.* Would you like me to call him for you?"

"Not necessary," Travis said. "But thanks." He'd look Rico up himself as soon as he got Julie settled in one of the penthouse suites always kept in reserve for visiting family.

"Hello," Julie interrupted. "I'm Julie O'—King." She held out one hand to the doorman, and he took it, surprised a little that she would take the time to introduce herself.

Travis frowned a little and she gave him a

smile that told him she wasn't going to be ignored. He imagined the cameramen stationed out in front of the gates were now busily clicking off shots of he and Julie together. And they probably didn't look real happy with each other.

That thought paramount in his mind, he took her elbow, nodded at the doorman and led her into the sanctuary of the hotel—away from prying camera lenses.

"That was rude," she muttered, pulling her elbow from his grasp.

"I don't ordinarily introduce my companions to the doorman," Travis muttered and laid his hand on the small of her back.

"God, you're a snob."

"I'm *not* a snob," he whispered, irritated at the jab. "But Esteban has his job and he doesn't expect to be pals with the guests."

"I didn't say I wanted to have lunch with him, but he knew *you*. No reason why he couldn't know who I am." Her heels clicked musically on the polished marble floor until she stopped abruptly. "Unless of course, you're ashamed of me."

"Hmm," he mused, stopping alongside her. "Ashamed of being married to a bigamist. Why would that bother me? I wonder…"

Her eyes narrowed on him and her jaw went tight. "That wasn't my fault."

"So you keep saying." He glanced around and caught the eye of several people watching him and Julie with open curiosity. Perfect.

He lowered his voice even further. "I'd appreciate it if you'd just keep a low profile until things are cleared up."

"Ah. Low profile? Like the stretch limo?"

He blew out a breath and looked at her. Her grass-green eyes were practically snapping with nerves and anger. Her mouth was tight, and her chin was lifted in defiance. Her breath rushed in and out of her lungs and her breasts strained against the deep vee neckline of her dark green dress.

She looked ready for battle and so damned edible, his body went hard as a rock almost instantly.

A sex-free year with a woman who managed to turn him on even when he was furious.

Damn it.

"Look," he said, forcing a smile so no one in the lobby would guess that he and his new bride were ready to shout at each other. "We don't need to announce our presence, all right? Let's do what we're here to do and move on."

"I'm just saying, I won't be ignored."

"Fine. Point taken."

"Good." Now she smiled, curving that luscious mouth up at the corners. Only he was close enough to see that there was no answering warmth in her eyes.

Muttering vicious curses under his breath about marrying women he couldn't sleep with and couldn't kill, Travis hooked her arm through his and continued on to the reservations desk. A young woman with dark brown hair piled atop her head smiled at him.

"Señor King." She practically purred his name and beside him, Travis felt Julie stiffen.

"Welcome back to the Castello," the clerk continued, dismissing Julie with hardly more than a glance. "We have the room ready for you and your…companion. As you requested."

"Thanks, Olympia." He was polite, but completely uninterested in whatever other games she might be playing. Travis wasn't an idiot. He knew women were drawn to money and power and he'd been flirted with by the best. He'd also learned long ago that the best way to handle the situation was to simply ignore it.

The woman's coy smile and big brown eyes

might have worked on any other man, but
Travis was immune.

"Do you know everyone here?" Julie whispered as she leaned in close to his ear.

He smiled as if she'd said something
tempting, then leaned back and murmured,
"She's wearing a name tag."

"Oh."

"Will you be needing reservations at the res-
taurant this evening?" The woman still
avoided looking at Julie, instead giving Travis
alone the benefit of her wide-eyed stare.

"No, thanks," he said, tapping his fingertips
as he waited to sign for the room.

"And your...*companion,*" she asked
quietly. "Will she be staying with you for
your entire visit?"

"What?"

"Yes," Julie said for him, leaning one arm
on the reservations desk as she glared at the

girl now watching her warily. "I *will* be here for his entire visit, since I'm not his 'companion,' but his *wife*."

"I see," the girl muttered, hurrying now with the details of check-in.

Travis bit the inside of his cheek and enjoyed the show as Julie set the little flirt down flat. There was something damned attractive about watching her sail into battle. And he couldn't help admiring the fact that she wasn't afraid to stand up for herself.

"And no," Julie said firmly. "We won't be needing your assistance with a reservation, thank you *so* much."

"Of course, señora," the girl whispered, ducking her head to avoid the icicles shooting out of Julie's green eyes.

Her point made, Julie's voice softened. "Now, if you don't mind, we're on our honeymoon and we'd like to get to our room." Then she leaned into Travis and ran her fingers over the front of his shirt for good measure.

And just like that, every last drop of amusement drained out of his body to be replaced with a heat that was powerful enough to make his eyes glaze over. Even though he knew she was putting on a performance, Travis hissed in a breath as his body tightened even further. Damn, if she kept this up, he was going to have a hard time walking to the elevator.

He looked down into her green eyes, and noted that she was completely aware of what she was doing to him. She ran the tip of her tongue over her bottom lip and everything in him fisted. What the hell game was she playing?

Sliding a glance at the clerk again, Julie smiled and said on a sigh, "I'm sure you understand that we're anxious to be…alone."

"Yes, yes of course." The last of the girl's flirtatious attitude disappeared and she hurried through the rest of the paperwork.

Julie was still plastering herself to his side and Travis told himself that two could play this game. Once he'd signed in and received his key, he wrapped his arms around her, dragged her in tight and kissed her hard and fast.

That kiss sizzled through his bloodstream, tightened his erection to the bursting point and left Julie speechless. Objective attained.

"Thanks," he said, nodding at the clerk before leading Julie toward the elevator.

Julie's mouth was still burning an hour later.

As if she could still feel Travis's lips pressed to hers.

Fine, she hadn't liked the way that woman at the desk had been leering at Travis as if Julie weren't standing right beside him. Although, maybe she shouldn't have laid it on so thick after shutting the girl down. Teasing Travis was something like waving a raw steak in front of a hungry lion. Not surprising then that he'd kissed her in response. What *was* surprising was the quicksilver flash of heat and need that had rushed through her the moment his mouth claimed hers.

Had he felt it, too?

Or had he just been pretending?

Of course he was, she chided herself silently. He was playing his part and doing a darn fine job of it, too. She tried to concentrate on the task at hand, but once she was finished unpacking her clothes, she was free again to think about things she really shouldn't be even considering.

But could she help it if her body was on fire?

Oh, boy. She might be in some serious trouble.

Leaving the smaller of the two bedrooms in the luxurious suite, she walked into the living room and paused on the threshold just to admire the view. The room was wide and long, decorated with sheer elegance. Four low-slung white couches formed a circle around a fireplace set in the middle of the room in a stone ring. A huge flatscreen television hung on one wall. On the far side of the room, was a massive wet bar and accompanying wine cooler, and beautiful paintings adorned the rest of the soft yellow walls.

Brightly colored rugs were scattered across the glossy, honey-colored wood floor, and terrace doors leading to a balcony almost as big as her bedroom stood wide open. A cool breeze blew in from the nearby ocean and carried both the scent of the sea and the fragrance of the tropical flowers that surrounded this amazing hotel.

Standing on the terrace, Travis waited, his back to her and their room. Looking him up and down, she fought the swirl of attraction she felt. It wasn't easy. He'd discarded his suit jacket and tie and now wore only his slacks and a crisp white shirt. His dark hair ruffled in the breeze as he poured two glasses of champagne from the bottle chilling in what was probably a sterling silver ice bucket.

Steeling herself, Julie lifted her chin and started forward, the sound of her heels on the floor the only sound in the room. She stepped out onto the terrace and instantly felt the cool wind surround her. Goose bumps lifted on her arms, but she paid no attention. Instead, she focused on the lights below and the darkening sky above.

"Unpacked?" Travis asked.

"Yes," she said, accepting the champagne flute he handed her and taking a sip. The margaritas she'd had on the plane were still with her and she really should eat something before she had anything else to drink. But she glanced down at the munchies he'd ordered from room service and knew she couldn't swallow anything else at the moment. "It's a beautiful place."

"Yeah, it is."

"I guess you come here often," she said.

He shrugged. "It's a family hotel. Everyone comes here often."

"Uh-huh," she said, with another sip of the bubbly wine. "And I'm guessing you usually have a 'companion' with you?"

"Jealous?" he asked, turning his head to look at her. One dark eyebrow was arched and the wind in his hair gave him a softer, more vulnerable look.

Travis King?

Vulnerable?

"No, I'm not jealous," she said. "That would be silly, wouldn't it? It's not like we're actually—"

"Married?" His smile disappeared in a blink. "No, guess we're not. Which is why we're here. And on that subject, I'll talk to my cousin Rico tomorrow. Get the bead on who we should go to about arranging this divorce."

"Great." She walked toward the iron railing and laid one hand on the cool surface. Taking another drink of the champagne, Julie was aware that the bubbles were going directly to her head, but maybe that was a good thing.

"You're a good actress, I give you that," Travis pointed out.

"Hmm?"

"The performance you put on for the clerk downstairs almost had me convinced you were a happy newlywed."

"Yeah, well," she said, wondering why her glass was empty just before Travis reached out and refilled it. "She ticked me off."

"I guessed that much."

"And you enjoyed it," she said, taking another sip, allowing the bubbles to slide down her throat and buzz through her blood.

"I did," he said, draining his own glass of champagne in one long swallow. He refilled his glass and took another sip before speaking again. "Had to wonder, though."

"What?" God, it felt good to be out here, feeling the wind on her skin and the champagne in her blood. Looking at Travis, she felt a warmth, too. A sort of heat that was settling down low inside her. Danger, Julie. *Oh, be quiet,* she ordered that annoying internal voice.

"Well, that acting skill of yours," he said, coming around the tiny table to stand beside her.

Julie drained her champagne and licked her lips as her body began to hum. She wasn't drunk, but she was feeling pretty good. "What about it?"

"If you're that good at acting, maybe you've been playing me all along."

She blew out a breath in frustration. If he was going to continue to believe that she was in cahoots with Jean Claude then this year was going to be misery.

"I told you Travis, I wouldn't do that." She set her glass down onto the table.

"I'd like to believe you, Julie," he was saying, reaching out with a finger to play with one of the straps of her dress. "But—"

"But?" How could he really believe that about her and still want her? More, how could she be burning up with lust for him, knowing that he thought her capable of blackmail?

Apparently, though, her mind and her body were riding two different tracks. Her skin felt as if it was on fire where he was touching her. Nerves rattled through Julie's body and she knew she was in big trouble. But she didn't care.

"I'm thinking I need some convincing," he said, his dark eyes flashing with a need that her body was clamoring to answer.

"I don't know what more I can say."

"No more talking," he said and set his glass down on the table beside hers.

"Then what…"

He slid one of her dress straps down her shoulder and smoothed his thumb over her skin. Her gaze locked with his, Julie's breath caught and her blood began to pump thick and hot and urgent.

"I paid a hundred thousand dollars to marry you today," Travis said, dipping his head to kiss her bare shoulder.

Julie sucked in a gulp of air.

"Now," he said, straightening up as his finger slid along the line of her bodice, dipping down to caress the valley between her breasts. "How about you show me what I paid for?"

Five

Julie just stared at him for what felt like forever. Shock had her feeling a little stunned, but as she looked at him, she sensed that he was waiting for her response. To see if she'd take this or stand up and call him on it.

He didn't have to wait long.

His gaze was dark and hot and spearing into hers, daring her to look away. She didn't. Instead, she pulled in a deep breath, kept her gaze locked with his and said too sweetly, "Since you actually paid the hundred thousand dollars to Jean Claude…why don't I call him for you and *he* can show you whatever you like?"

Amusement flickered in Travis's eyes and one corner of his mouth lifted. "Good one. But I'm not interested in your Frenchman."

Frustration bubbled up inside her, frothier than the champagne she'd just drunk way too much of. "For heaven's sake, he's not *my* French—" She stopped because the amusement in his eyes was even brighter now. Frustration gave way to confusion. "You're laughing?"

"Not laughing, smiling."

"About?"

"About how we ended up here together, despite your Frenchman—"

She opened her mouth to protest, but he cut her off quickly. "And how we've both had too much to drink," he continued. "And how you smell so good it's driving me nuts."

Her nipples peaked.

For pity's sake, he didn't even have to *try* and her body jumped and cheered.

"Plus—" he added, dipping his index finger into the valley between her breasts again "—you look beautiful. This dress…is amazing. It tempts me to peel it off you and discover all your secrets."

She trembled. He was too close. Too warm. His breath was too soft on her face and the fire in his eyes was like an incendiary, quickening a similar blaze inside her.

When he wasn't trying to seduce her, he was nearly irresistible. When he *was* trying, he was downright illegal. His finger stroked the tops of her breasts and Julie's already fuzzy brain started clouding up completely.

"Um, Travis?" Her mouth was dry and her breath was coming in tight, short gasps that were really contributing to the whole light-headed thing.

"Yeah?" He kissed her shoulder again.

Oh, he had a great mouth.

"Um…" She was really trying to think, but it was suddenly so hard. Her nerve endings were lit up like a marquee in Las Vegas and her core was damp and hot and oh, so achingly ready that her brain probably figured it wouldn't be required anymore that night, so it had shut down.

Still, Julie tried to think. She couldn't quite remember what it was that had seemed so important a moment ago. His lips and tongue moved on her bare shoulder, the edges of his teeth scraping against her skin, sending shockwaves pulsing throughout her system. Like the aftershocks of an earthquake, everything seemed just a little off-kilter.

But at last, a solitary wispy thought flashed across her mind and Julie grabbed for it. "Right. Right, Travis…"

"Mmm…" He kissed the side of her neck and Julie tipped her head to one side to make sure he covered every square inch of available skin.

"We, uh, we agreed," she said, struggling for air while trying desperately to hold onto that one tiny thought. "Agreed to a no-sex policy for this marriage. Remember?"

"Nope," he whispered, kissing the base of her neck until Julie's toes curled. "Don't remember a thing."

Was that his tongue on her neck now? Licking, tasting. Oh, my. "It was uh…in the uh…" What was that thing called again? "*Contract!* That's it. It was in the contract."

His fingertips smoothed over the tops of her breasts and her nipples popped even harder, each of them eagerly awaiting his attentions.

"We can always renegotiate a contract," he said, sliding his free hand up her bare back to the nape of her neck. His fingers rubbed and stroked, and slid into her hair. "If we want to…."

She groaned and closed her eyes, relishing

the feel of him all around her. His body was pressed close and his erection straining against her hip was unmistakable. One hand on her breasts, the other stroking her neck, her back, he was overwhelming her with sensation. Short-circuiting her mind with deliciously seductive maneuvers that left her breathless.

"Oh, boy." She took a breath, forcing it into lungs straining for air, and when she blew it out again, she opened her eyes and looked at him. He lifted his head, his dark brown eyes locked on hers with a burning intensity she'd never seen before and she felt the heat as those flames reached for her, engulfed her. "Do we want to?" she asked. "Renegotiate, I mean?"

"Oh," he said, sliding his hand from the base of her neck all the way down her spine to the curve of her bottom. Rubbing, stroking, he leaned in and kissed her, then smoothed the tip of his tongue across her bottom lip before easing back to meet her gaze again. "I really think we do."

"Okay then," she whispered, moving against him, letting him feel that she was as electrified as he. That she wanted him as much as he wanted her. "Let's…negotiate."

"Right." He kissed her, slid the straps of her dress down and freed her breasts to his hungry gaze. Cold sea air touched her skin and Julie shivered, but it had nothing to do with the temperature. Every cell in her body was eagerly awaiting what came next.

When he cupped her breasts in his palms and bent to take her nipple into his mouth, he murmured, "Here's my first offer…."

Julie hissed in air through gritted teeth, and held on to Travis's shoulders as if without that stability she might just slide off the face of the earth. But she would die happy if he only kept his mouth right where it was.

As soon as that thought arrived though, he

stopped, lifted his head and said, "Inside. Let's take this inside."

"What? What?"

He glanced around as if just remembering where they were. "You never know just how sneaky photographers can get and I'd rather not see us on the front page, if you know what I mean."

Her eyes went wide as she covered her bare breasts with her arms and scuttled back into the hotel suite. Back against the wall, she waited while Travis closed the French doors and then swept the sheers shut with a yank on the cord.

"Oh, my God," she whispered, gaze locked on him. "Do you really think someone was out there…watching us? Taking pictures?"

He shrugged, but his eyes were cold and dark, belying his easy dismissal of the notion. "You never know."

"That's just—" She blew out a breath and tried to struggle back into her dress as if covering her breasts now could somehow erase their earlier exposure.

"Pointless to worry about," Travis told her gently. "My fault, I should have been more careful." He stroked his hand along her shoulder, stopping her from dragging the dress straps back up. "But you tasted so good. You smell so wonderful. Look so…"

Julie's body fired up again as if there hadn't been an interruption. She leaned back into the wall as Travis bent his head, taking first one nipple, then the other into his mouth. Sliding his tongue across the sensitive tip, suckling, nibbling. He tormented her with tenderness. Conquered her defenses with gentle deliberation. And when she was gasping for air and wobbling in place, he stood up, took her mouth with his and sent her flying again.

His tongue tangled with hers and everything within her went hot and wild. Her core became a molten ache, desperate to have him inside. Her hips twisted against his, and his erection pressed tight and hard to her body, letting her know that he was as hungry, as frenzied as she.

How was this possible, she wondered frantically. How could she feel so much for a man she'd known her whole life? How was there this much passion in someone she'd considered a friend? How could she slip so totally into complete abandon at his touch?

Then she stopped thinking. Stopped wondering. Instead, she surrendered to the magic rising up between them.

He wrapped a hand around the base of her neck and tipped her head to one side. He nibbled his way down the length of her throat, and then slid back up, leaving a trail of damp heat behind him as he kissed and licked her skin. She was struggling for air, but not really concerned. Who needed to breathe when there was all of *this* to feel?

But she wanted more. Needed more. Needed to feel his skin beneath her hands. Needed to touch as she was touched. Feel as she was felt.

Sliding her hands up his chest, she tore at the buttons on his dress shirt until she'd freed them all, sending several of them pinging to the floor. Then she was touching his hard, muscled skin, feeling the soft curl of dark brown hair beneath her fingers and dragging her nails across his flat nipples.

He growled in her ear and took her mouth harder, deeper. Their breaths mingled, their tongues played out a dance their bodies hungered for.

"I want you. Now." His voice was harsh, strained as if it were all he could do to squeeze out those few words. Then Travis reached down, lifted the skirt of her dress and ripped her tiny lace panties from her body.

Julie inhaled sharply and then groaned as he

cupped her aching core. Sliding first one, then two fingers into her depths, he pushed her so high, so fast, her head spun. As his fingers delved inside her, his tongue continued to twist with hers in a frantic dance of need and passion.

Her body coiled tight as he rubbed one sensitive spot over and over and Julie's legs trembled violently as she tried desperately to keep her balance while giving herself over to the incredible sensations shooting through her. Again and again, he stroked her, pushing her as if he couldn't wait to feel her climax.

But she fought the feeling, wanting to draw this out as long as she could. Incredible, the way he made her feel. Overwhelming, the way she wanted him, needed him. She'd never known anything even remotely like this before and she wanted more of it. Her hands dropped to his waist and her fingers fumbled with his belt, then the snap and zipper of his slacks.

He broke their kiss as she wrapped her hand

around him. His eyes briefly slid shut and he ground out one word. Her name. "Julie…"

"I want you to feel what I feel," she whispered, opening her eyes and looking into his. Raw passion and desire shone out at her and she knew he must be seeing the same things reflected back at him. She was on fire for him, her body burning inside and out. As if a fever were raging through her system.

She stroked him, her fingertips sliding up and down his length, stroking the sensitive tip of him, marveling at the soft strength of him. Travis went completely still for one long, shattering minute when their ragged breaths were the only sound in the room other than the quiet hiss and snap of the fire.

Then he looked down at her, shifted his hands to her waist and said, "Lift your legs."

She didn't ask why. Didn't think. Just went with what she was feeling, needing. Lifting her legs, she wrapped them around his hips and he leaned into her, bracing her back against the wall, cupping his hands on her bottom.

And in the next moment, he was sliding inside her, pushing himself into her body.

"Oh, Travis…" Julie sighed, twisted her hips, writhed on him as she took every amazing inch of him. An invasion of the most amazing kind, she thought, relishing the feel of his body filling hers.

He groaned tightly and began to move, slowly at first, then with a soul-splintering speed that had his hips pistoning against hers. Their bodies met and separated over and over as tension coiled and need escalated.

She felt it building, knew her release was so close she could almost touch it. The tingling sensations soared and a delicious ache rose inside until it was nearly unbearable. His strength surrounded her, his body filled her and he didn't stop. Couldn't stop. She moved with him, her body welcoming his, holding him tightly, creating a fabulous friction that accelerated the desire clawing at them both.

And when the first tiny explosions shattered within her, Julie's eyes flew open so that she could look at Travis as her body exploded in a shower of light and color and sensation like she'd never known before. His gaze was dark, hot, steady.

"Let go," he whispered.

And she did.

"Travis!" She held on to him, arms locked around his neck, legs crossed at his spine. She pulled him in tighter, closer, holding him to her as an enormous wave of pleasure crested inside her.

Her climax pushed him over that teetering edge of control and before the last of the sweeping tide of ripples had died away, Travis called her name on a hoarse shout of victory and emptied himself into her.

When the storm was over, Travis's blood

was still pumping like fury through his veins. He'd thought having her would clear his head, make the wanting less, the attraction he'd felt for her less powerful.

Big mistake.

Julie nestled against him, laying her head on his shoulder and he wanted her all over again. Her heat, her touch, her explosive reaction to his lovemaking all combined to only feed the fires already quickening inside him. He hadn't eased the desire he felt for her, he'd only fed the flames.

He turned his face toward her, kissed her forehead and murmured, "I'm not done."

She lifted her head, kissed him lightly, briefly and whispered, "Me, neither."

In an instant, his body thickened inside hers, tightening, hardening. She shifted in his arms, wiggling her hips and everything in him fisted hard and tight. He wanted her. More than he had before.

Turning, he held her close, their bodies still joined, he took the few steps to the nearest couch and laid her down. Beside them, the fire burned, and light and shadow played across her features in a never-ending shift of patterns that only served to make her more beautiful, more dreamlike.

Travis wanted nothing between them this time. He slid free of her body long enough to tear his clothes off, then he bent down over her and helped her shimmy out of her dress. Then she was naked, lying on the soft, pale fabric of the couch and lifting her arms to him.

"Do it again, Travis," she whispered as he came into her embrace. "Take me there again and let me take you."

He didn't need to be asked twice.

Covering her with his body, he braced his weight on his hands at either side of her head. Her eyes were wide and shining in the firelight, the deep green sparkling with a golden glow that intrigued and captivated him. Her mouth was swollen from his kisses and when she touched the tip of her tongue to her lips, he bent his head to capture it.

Their mouths fused as he entered her on a slow slide of languorous satisfaction. He pushed himself into her heat with a calm deliberation he wasn't really feeling. Every instinct had him clamoring to take her, to drive himself into her body, but his will kept him moving slowly, drawing out the pleasure, making each inch of her he claimed a small victory.

"Travis—" She tore her mouth from his and sucked in air desperately. Lifting her hips under him, she sought to take him in more fully, to draw him deep, high inside. "I need…I need…"

"Me, too." His words were strained, hollow, echoing with the desperation suddenly tearing at him. With each of her movements, she tore at the foundations of his self-control, his will.

He hadn't expected this lightninglike connection between them. Now, he couldn't imagine doing without it.

Travis felt her body tighten around his, felt the first velvety grip of her inner muscles and watched as her eyes flashed with wonder. Then he let himself go, falling into the green of her eyes and the warmth of her body.

The next morning, Julie was feeling completely sated and impossibly lazy. Her body ached in a very good way and just for a second or two, she stretched on the bed and let herself remember the night before.

Lying in Travis's arms. Feeling the magic that sprung up between them when they touched. Experiencing the incredible sensations caused when their bodies joined. And just for that second or two, she allowed herself to pretend that this marriage was real. That they'd really found something amazing together.

But in the next moment, that illusion was shattered.

"I don't *believe* this!" Travis's outraged shout carried from the next room.

She bolted up in the oversized bed in his room and scrambled off the mattress. Naked, she stood there for a second, wishing she had her robe. Then she shrugged and dragged a sheet they'd yanked loose during the night around her body. Tripping on the edges of it as she went, Julie stumbled into the main room.

Travis was still as a statue, standing in a wide splash of sunlight pouring through the open French doors. A room service cart loaded down with coffee, fresh fruits and an assortment of breakfast pastries stood unnoticed beside him. He held a newspaper and his features were filled with fury as he stared at the front page.

"Travis?"

His gaze snapped to hers and she watched as the anger in his eyes shifted to a different, much harder to read emotion. "We've got a situation."

"Yeah, I heard," she said, tugging the sheet out of her way as she walked toward him. "What's wrong?"

"What isn't?" When she was close enough, he turned the paper toward her.

"Oh, my G—" With her free hand, she snatched at the newspaper and tilted it so that the black-and-white picture taking up most of the front page was in the sunlight. But she hadn't really needed clarification.

The headline was large and black. *King and His New Queen.* She winced at that and wondered idly if that would be her new nickname in the press. But when she glanced farther down and took in the picture below the headline, the title *Queen* was the least of her worries.

The photograph was crystal clear and so detailed, the photographer might as well have been in the room with them. Or rather, on the terrace.

There she and Travis were, captured in the moment when desire had leaped up between them. Her head was thrown back in ecstasy as his hands cupped her breasts and his mouth was at her throat.

They looked like an X-rated version of a vampire and his victim. Thank heaven the newspaper had thoughtfully provided a black bar across her naked breasts.

How very classy of them.

Oh, God, would her *mother* see this? Embarrassment flooded her body and she felt the heat of it swamp through her like a brushfire rushing uphill. Her gaze lifted to his. "I can't believe this."

"Welcome to my world," he muttered, then shoved one hand through his thick, dark hair.

Half turning, he poured them each a cup of steaming coffee and handed one to her.

"Damn photographers." He shook his head grimly, took a sip of coffee and said, "This is my fault, Julie. I shouldn't have taken the chance of being seen, but I was caught off guard and—"

"We both were," she murmured, shifting her gaze back to the photo of Travis nibbling at her throat. She could hardly swallow her own coffee and was half afraid that the jolt of caffeine would only clear up her vision, making the photo even worse.

"Yes, but you're not used to life in the spotlight. I should have been thinking. Should have remembered telephoto lenses, damn it."

Looking up at him, Julie saw that he was both furious and frustrated. Probably not a good combination. "Wasn't your fault, Travis. Besides, it doesn't matter now how it happened. The point is, it *did.* Can't you—"

she shook the paper, then tossed it to the table and concentrated on her coffee "—sue them or something?"

"Pointless," he said darkly. "It only revs up interest. If we're lucky, this will stay in the local paper and not be picked up by the bigger outlets."

"Yeah," she said, closing her eyes briefly. "I feel lucky."

He snapped her a look and seemed to notice what she was wearing—or more precisely, what she *wasn't* wearing. Moving to the French doors, he closed them, then yanked the sheers closed across them. "No more gifts to the paparazzi," he said.

"Right." She clutched her sheet tighter with one hand and held on to her coffee with the other. "So, what're we going to do about all of this?"

"I'll have my lawyers contact the paper here in town—"

"But I thought suing was—"

"Not for a suit. He'll pull out the legalese and give them a stern lecture though."

Oh, yeah, she'd always figured that paparazzi could be tamed if someone would just sit down and give them a good talking to. But no point throwing a metaphorical log onto his fire. "And then?"

"Then…" He checked his gold wristwatch. "I'm meeting my cousin Rico in a half hour. He's got some ideas on a few judges I can talk to about getting your prior marriage dissolved quickly and quietly."

"Okay," Julie said, already walking toward her half of the suite. "Give me fifteen minutes. I'll be showered, dressed and ready."

"No need," he said brusquely, topping off his coffee. "You just sit tight. I'll take care of the arrangements."

"Sit tight?" she echoed, disbelief coloring her tone.

"Yeah." He walked to a nearby table, picked up a remote and punched a button. The big-screen television flickered to life. "Rent movies, have a massage, go to the pool. Or, there's a shopping pavilion on the ground floor. Go buy things."

Julie stared at him, amazed. He actually thought that she would trot off and play lazy rich wife while he was out dealing with her past and arranging her future? Oh, that was never going to happen.

"Uh-huh," she said. "Shopping. Massage. Is that how the other women you've brought here spent their time?"

He must have caught something in her tone because he swiveled his head to look at her, confusion clearly stamped on his face. "Yes," he admitted. "They all seemed to enjoy themselves. Why wouldn't you?"

All of them?

Of course, *all,* she told herself. Travis had probably brought dozens of women to this hotel. This suite. They'd all romped in that bed with him and— Oh, she so didn't want to think about that right now.

No wonder the desk clerk had tried her hand at a little seduction. From her point of view, Julie was no more than the latest female in a long, staggering line of Travis's companions.

Well, Julie was different. She might not be the woman of his dreams, but for now anyway, she was at least his *wife*. Well, more or less. And she wouldn't be treated like some brainless bimbo looking to get a tight grip on his credit cards.

"I didn't come here to shop. Or to get a massage. Or to do any number of the things your usual women are so entertained by," she reminded him. "I'm here to straighten out a mistake in my past."

"It's being handled," he said, glancing back at the television where a space battle was taking place in showering sparks and flashing lights.

"By you."

"Yes, by me."

Julie stared at him. "But this doesn't just concern you, Travis. This is about *me.*"

"Julie, you're making too much of this. You're tired and frustrated and I'm sure the wake-up call in the paper has you upset, too."

She could almost *feel* him giving her a pat on the head. She took a long deep breath and fanned the flames of her own simmering temper. "So what you're saying is, I should just stay here, out of the way and not worry my pretty little head about it?"

He finally seemed to catch the tone of her voice, then turned to her and frowned. "I didn't say that."

"You implied it."

"For God's sake, Julie…"

"Forget it, Travis," she said, heading for her bedroom and the shower. "You may have thought you were getting yourself a temporary mousey wife, but you got one with a mind of her own."

"You'll only complicate matters," he called after her.

She stopped in the doorway to her bedroom and looked back over her shoulder at him. "Let's remember, I trusted Jean Claude to get that divorce without my input. Just look how well that turned out."

"I'm not Pierre."

"No, you're not," she said, hitching the sheet a little higher across her breasts. She felt like an idiot having this conversation while wearing nothing but a silken bed sheet. "You're Travis King, used to getting his own way and having people shout 'how high?' when you say 'jump.' Just so you know, I don't jump. Ever. So if you think I'm going to trust another man to take care of something this important without my being involved, you're way wrong. I'll be ready in fifteen minutes."

Six

"There's a car waiting for you outside. The driver will take you to Judge Hernandez."

Travis nodded. His cousin Rico King stood out in the glossy, airy lobby of his hotel like Death come to a wedding. In the middle of pale pastels and bright tropical colors, Rico wore his preferred black. Black long-sleeved shirt, black jeans, black boots. His black hair hung over his collar and his dark eyes were, at the moment, amused.

"Something funny?" Travis asked.

"To see you with a bride—" Rico said, shrugging "—entertains me."

"Happy to help," Travis muttered and slanted a look at the glass-fronted gift store where Julie was buying a pack of gum before their trip to the judge's office. He hadn't been able to change her mind and she'd been so fast at showering and getting ready, he hadn't been able to leave before her, either. Besides, knowing Julie, she simply would have followed after him if he'd tried.

She was wearing a soft yellow dress with spaghetti straps and a slightly flared skirt. Her long legs were bare and golden and looked great thanks to the towering beige high heels she wore. In a second, his mind shot back to the night before, when those long legs of hers had been locked around his hips and just like that, Travis's body was hot and needy again.

"Your bride is a beauty," Rico said.

Travis frowned. "Yeah. I guess so."

"You guess?" Rico slapped his back. "Let me assure you that if you're regretting your hasty marriage, I'd be happy to console your grieving spouse."

The thought of Rico anywhere near Julie made temper spike inside him. "Leave her alone."

His cousin chuckled. "Do I sense a territorial streak?"

"You sense my wife. Now cut it out."

"Of course." Rico held both hands up in surrender. "My mistake."

Travis sucked in air and blew it out in a rush. As Julie walked toward them smiling, he told himself he wasn't being territorial. Though he did notice the eyes of several of the men in the lobby following Julie's progress across the shining floor. He was only playing his role as devoted husband.

That was all.

* * *

She didn't speak Spanish, Travis thought. The one saving grace in all of this.

Julie might have insisted on accompanying him, but at least she was forced to stay out of the conversation he had with a local judge. Though the man probably spoke English, Travis immediately insisted on Spanish. Not that he wasn't interested in Julie's suggestions. Actually, he wasn't. He wanted to take care of this on his own.

Rico had assured Travis that with a few donations in the right quarters, his problems could be solved very quickly and discretely. Travis could appreciate that. Hell, all over the world, money solved problems faster than anything else.

By the time he had Judge Hernandez's promise of a swift resolution to their problem, Julie was shifting impatiently in her chair and peppering him with questions.

"What was that?" She tugged at his jacket sleeve to get his attention, as if he couldn't hear her. "What did he say? Does he think he can arrange the divorce? Will he marry us? Why doesn't he speak English? People in California speak Spanish."

"You don't," Travis reminded her, with a smile for the judge.

"I could have," she muttered. "I just didn't pay attention in high school."

"Unfortunate for you."

"*¿Qué?*" The judge interrupted, a question in his eyes.

Travis took Julie's arm, drew her to her feet and in Spanish, assured the judge that all was well and that they would be at Castello de King waiting to hear from him.

They took the elevator to the street level lobby and stepped out onto a crowded thoroughfare. Sunlight stabbed down from a cloudless blue sky, glanced off the asphalt and simmered in the air.

Tourists and locals alike jammed the side-walks and streets. Cars were practically at a standstill as people wandered in and out of shops, back and forth across the road and stopped at carts to buy everything from hats and scarves to tacos and churros, Mexican pastries rolled in cinnamon and sugar. The sounds and scents of the resort town were overwhelming.

But not to Julie.

"Tell me everything he said," she demanded.

The woman was single-minded if nothing else.

"Judge Hernandez is on it," Travis told her, gripping her elbow to steer her through the crowds. "Money talks here as well as it does at home."

"So you *bribed* him?" Shock colored her tone.

"No." He shot her a frown and shook his head. "I'm not bribing anyone. It's just that if you've got enough money to back you up, you can make the wheels turn a little faster."

"Okay. So did he say how long it would take?"

"No." Travis scowled again and stepped around a man wearing at least fifteen wide-brimmed hats on his head while he did some fast sales pitch to the people streaming past him. "But Rico figures two weeks."

"Two weeks?"

"Is there a problem?"

"No," she said, hurrying her steps to keep up with his much longer strides. "I just didn't know we'd be gone so long. Don't you have to work on that distribution deal with Thomas Henry?"

"Yes." And he didn't like the thought of putting it off. But better to have this marriage-divorce-remarriage thing taken care of before dealing with Henry. "He expects us to have a honeymoon, though."

"Honeymoon." She stumbled on a crack in

the sidewalk and Travis tightened his grip on her. "So what are we really going to be doing?"

He stopped and held his ground as pedestrians slammed into him from all sides. Perfect zone for a pickpocket, he knew, so he glanced around before looking into her eyes. When he did, he heard his cousin's voice echoing in his head.

Your bride is a beauty.

She really was. Funny, but until recently, he'd always seen her as just Julie. Someone he'd known forever. Someone he once climbed trees with. After last night though, he doubted he'd ever see her as a kid again. And with that thought in mind, a slow and sure smile formed on his lips.

"We have a honeymoon."

"Are you serious?"

"Why not?" He said it with a shrug, then pulled her out of the flow of foot traffic to stand in the shade of a T-shirt shop. "We're in one of the most romantic places in the world and I think we proved last night that we're *compatible*."

"But what about our agreement?"

"Already gone, isn't it?" He smiled again and stroked the tip of one finger along her jawline. He didn't know what he'd been thinking to propose a year of no sex with a woman who could turn him on with a glance. "Look," he said softly. "We crossed over the line last night. Any real reason we ought to go back?"

"I suppose not...."

"Thanks for the enthusiasm."

"No, it's not that." She looked around, then shifted her gaze back to his. "Travis, we need to talk about something. It didn't occur to me until this morning and then we had to rush out to meet the judge and it wasn't the right time to talk to you about it, but now that we're talking about *this,* then it's the right time to bring up the other."

"What?"

She blew out a breath that ruffled the dark red curls laying on her forehead. "Can we go somewhere a little less crowded?" Her big green eyes were focused on him and didn't look happy.

"Sure. Come on." Whatever it was, he wanted to hear her out and take care of it. No more problems. He grabbed her hand, and felt her fingers automatically entwine with his. Leading the way through the crowd, he pulled her in his wake until he spotted a small city park off to the right. He headed for it and didn't stop until they were sitting on a curved stone bench beneath a shade tree.

The sun was hot, but under the tree, the temperature dropped by at least fifteen degrees. The sounds of the nearby ocean thumped in the air like a heartbeat and birdsong played counterpoint to the bustle of the crowd just a few feet away.

"Okay. Less crowded," he said, turning to face her on the bench. "Let's hear it."

"You're not going to like it."

He would have been willing to bet money on that. "Just get it said."

"Fine," she blurted, sitting back against the bench. "We didn't use any protection last night."

He stared at her, waiting for her to laugh. To tell him she was kidding and of course there was no problem. When she didn't, he felt an invisible noose tighten around his neck, trying to shut off his air. "Protection? Aren't you on the Pill?"

She gaped at him. "No, I'm not on the Pill. Why would I be?"

Damn it. "I just assumed…"

Folding her arms across her chest, she tipped her head to one side and arched both eyebrows. "And why would you assume that?"

"Because." He jumped to his feet, walked a few paces, then spun around and came back.

Keeping his voice low, he snapped, "I figured you weren't interested in getting pregnant."

"Isn't that what condoms are for?"

Yes. And damned if he could even remember the last time he'd had unprotected sex. Travis was a careful man. He liked his life the way it was. His only commitment to his work. So when it came to his women, he practically sealed himself up with plastic wrap to avoid being caught by a woman looking for more than a brief sexual relationship.

So why the hell hadn't he thought of that last night?

Because he hadn't been thinking at all. He'd gone into this marriage regarding it as nothing more than an in-name-only bargain. They'd agreed to no sex, so he hadn't even considered that it would be an issue. Then last night, he'd let his hormones lead him down a path that was turning around now to bite him in the ass.

"Perfect," he muttered. "Just perfect."

"How do you think I feel?"

He looked at her, one eyebrow arching. "Interesting question. How *do* you feel? Happy? Excited? Visions of King bank accounts dancing in your head?"

"Excuse me?"

"Well come on, Julie," he said. "You wouldn't be the first woman to try this."

"Just hold on one minute there, buster."

"Buster?" One corner of his mouth lifted.

"If you think I did this on *purpose,* you're way off base."

"Is that right?"

"Of course it's right." She stood up, too, and jabbed his chest with the tip of her index finger. "I'm not one of the hordes of women scheming to trap Travis King into marriage. *You* came to *me,* remember?"

One second ticked by, and then another while Julie gritted her teeth and waited for him to be an even bigger jerk. Surprisingly enough, it didn't happen.

Travis shook his head, stared off at the fast-moving parade of pedestrians such a short distance away from them and then turned his gaze back to her. "You're right. I did come to you. And what happened last night was both our faults."

"Wow," Julie said softly. "I think we're having a moment, here."

His mouth quirked, but his eyes were flat and dark. "Doesn't change the fact that this is a serious situation."

"Why do you think I brought it up?" She'd been doing some private panicking for most of the day. What if she was pregnant? Then what would happen to their "temporary" marriage? No. She pushed those worries out of her mind and told herself to think positively.

When he didn't say anything, she took a breath and shook her head. "Look, we're worried about this for nothing. It was only the one time…."

"Four," he corrected.

"The one *night,*" she amended. "What are the chances?"

"Guess we'll find out," he muttered, then took her hand and started for the sidewalk again.

"Where are we going now?" she asked as she practically ran after him.

"The nearest drugstore," he said. "To stock up on condoms."

A week later, Julie shielded her eyes and craned her neck back to stare up at the sky. Threads of white clouds stretched across the wide, blue expanse and the red-and-yellow sail dipping and swaying in the air currents looked like a gigantic tropical bird.

Of course, this bird was her husband, who was parasailing. Travis's impulsiveness hadn't changed any from when he was a kid.

He still liked to try everything at least once. And as that thought shot through her mind, her insides melted, then heated up again.

In the last week, they'd put quite a dent in their condom supply. There'd been no reason to cling to a no-sex vow when both of them were more than eager to share their nights in Travis's huge bed. And just thinking about the hours spent with him was enough to make Julie curl her bare toes into the hot, white sand beneath her.

She knew she was getting in deeper and deeper, but she couldn't seem to help herself, and she would defy any other red-blooded woman to be any different. Travis King was a one-man hormonal treat. When he had his tremendous focus aimed on one particular woman, he was irresistible. He had sucked Julie into his world and she didn't know how she'd ever get out again.

As she realized that, she felt as if someone had dropped a cold stone on her heart. God, she was an idiot. Staring up at the sky and her husband doing twirls and somersaults in the air currents, Julie felt her own stomach spin. This was the *second* time she'd married only to regret it almost immediately.

Jean Claude had been a creep, no doubt. But at least she hadn't been completely out of her element in that relationship. With Travis, their worlds were so different, they were bound to collide soon. She was the daughter of his family's cook for heaven's sake. And Cinderella aside, these things rarely turned out well.

Plus, he'd had to placate a blackmailer because of her! No, she knew that sooner or later, there was a world of hurt waiting for her. Because despite knowing that she shouldn't, that there was absolutely no logical reason for her to allow herself to fall in love…it was already happening.

"Señora King?"

"Huh? What?" She tore her gaze from

Travis, who was getting lower and lower in the sky, to look up at a hotel employee wearing white slacks and a green-and-white tropical shirt. "I'm sorry. What?"

He smiled and Julie wondered if Travis's cousin Rico hired only *gorgeous* employees.

"There is a phone call for you, señora," he said and handed her a small satellite phone.

"Oh, thanks," she said, though she couldn't figure out who would be calling her here. "Hello?"

"Julie O'Hara King," her mother said in a tone Julie hadn't heard since she was sixteen and late for curfew. "Would you explain to me how a completely indecent photo of you and Travis ended up on the front page of the tabloid at my local grocery store?"

Oh, God.

"Thomas, I'll straighten this out as soon as I—we—get home," Travis was saying.

From Julie's perch on one of the sleek sofas in their suite, she turned her head to follow Travis's progress as he paced around the perimeter of the room. Ever since he'd landed and been told about the scandalous photo of them that had apparently been sold to an American tabloid, Travis had practically been foaming at the mouth.

She couldn't really blame him, though. As it was, Julie wanted to find a hole and crawl into it. Her *mother* had seen that picture. And her friends at home. And *their* parents. And strangers the world over were, even now, standing in grocery lines across the globe, looking at her blacked-out boobs.

She groaned.

"My lawyers are handling the situation," he insisted and Julie had the feeling that Thomas Henry, wine distributor, was less than impressed with Travis's assurances.

By the time Travis had returned, Julie had

fielded three more phone calls, though none of them had had quite the embarrassing punch of her mother's. Still, talking to Travis's brothers, not to mention his lawyer, about the photos had pretty much sapped whatever energy she'd had left.

How was she ever supposed to look people in the eye again? Maybe she wouldn't have to, she thought frantically. Maybe they could move. To Zimbabwe or something. Yes. That would work. Run and hide until the embarrassment faded away. Shouldn't take more than ten or twenty years.

They couldn't hide though. They had to go back to Birkfield. Which was why Travis was on the phone now with Thomas Henry, trying to smooth ruffled feathers. Though what Henry had to be ruffled about, Julie wasn't quite sure. It wasn't *him* splashed across papers, sharing space with stories about headless aliens and fifty-pound newborns.

Oh, God.

"Fine. I'll get in touch as soon as I'm home. We'll work this out, Thomas." Travis hung up and tossed the phone onto the nearest chair. "This is a mess."

"You think?"

He shot her a quelling look.

She gave him one right back. "Hey, I'm in those pictures, too, you know."

"Right, right." He nodded, stuffed his hands into his slacks pockets and walked toward her. "I don't like not having control. It's not natural."

"Welcome to the real world," she muttered.

"I'd rather have my own. Where *I* make the rules."

She knew that. It was in his nature to be in charge. To take care of things himself. To protect those he cared about. Not that she was putting herself in that very select crowd. This was just a special circumstance.

Time for a change of subject. "What did Mr. Henry have to say?"

Travis scrubbed one hand across the back of his neck. "I told you he was eccentric? Well, he's also conservative. Yeah, and don't ask me how he can be both. He just is."

"Okay…" Eccentric and conservative.

"Seeing that picture made him rethink doing business with King wines, but I think he's coming around. He admits that it's our honeymoon and hardly our fault!" Travis said as Julie took a tight rein on her runaway imagination. Pay attention, she told herself.

"If we could just settle this marriage thing and get back home, I could tie up a business deal with Henry before he has a chance to back out."

His features were tight and his eyes were narrowed as if he thought he could solve everything simply by concentrating hard enough. But for the moment, he was stalled.

The future he planned was hanging just out of reach and there was nothing he could do to hurry things along.

That knowledge had to be driving him crazy, Julie thought. A man like Travis wasn't used to waiting or having zero input on what happened to him.

"My lawyer's tracking down the photographer," Travis said tightly. "And he's got a call in to the tabloids, for all the good it'll do. Now that the picture's out there, it's going to be a lot harder to get rid of."

Great. Julie stood, faced him, then quietly wrapped her arms around his middle, laying her head on his chest.

Travis just stood there. "What's this for?"

She tipped her head back and gave him a tired smile. "I thought you could use a hug. And Lord knows, I sure could."

He sighed, then folded his arms around her. "Good point." As he smoothed his hands up and down her back, he said, "I'll take care of this, Julie."

"I know," she said softly, relishing the feel of his hard body pressed along hers. She shouldn't enjoy this so much, Julie told herself. She shouldn't get used to the feeling that it was she and Travis against the world. That the two of them were a team, united against all attackers.

Because to Travis, this team of theirs was temporary.

And when the game was over, she'd be nothing more than a memory for him.

Seven

Four days later, Julie's divorce came through.

That same afternoon, Travis arranged for a quiet marriage ceremony in Judge Hernandez's office. The service was brief and, thanks to the judge, safely away from the prying eyes of roving photographers.

With everything at last settled, Travis was anxious to get back to the winery. He had plenty of plans to put into motion and now that he was safely—*legally*—married, he wanted to get started. A car was called to pick them up at the hotel for the short trip to the airport, where a King jet was waiting.

Travis felt as though he were finally getting a tight grip on his universe again. He was back at the helm and now that he'd taken care of the problems facing them, everything else was sure to run smoothly. He and Julie were working well together—who would have guessed he'd find the most incredible sexual partner in his life by marrying an old friend?

Turning his head slightly, he looked at her and tried to see past the instant jolt of pure lust that slammed into him. She was beautiful, true. But was she all that she claimed? There remained a niggling doubt deep within him that perhaps Julie wasn't as innocent as she professed to be. There'd just been too many things that had gone wrong since they'd married. Jean Claude. The photos of them on their balcony. The night they'd lost control and risked pregnancy.

He'd like to think that he could trust her. But the bottom line was, Julie had entered into this "marriage" for the same reasons he had. She was being paid well for participating and who was to say she hadn't cut a side deal with Jean Claude to try to improve on the one she'd already made with Travis?

When she turned her head to look up at him and smile, Travis told himself he had nothing to worry about. But still, he'd be cautious. It didn't pay to trust the wrong people.

He checked his watch and said, "If Rico doesn't get his butt out here soon, we're going to leave without saying goodbye."

"Five minutes, Travis," she said. "Relax."

But that wasn't going to happen anytime soon.

Still, he couldn't help admiring the woman he'd married, from a purely objective perspective, of course. She was wearing white slacks, a pale yellow tank top with a peach-colored overshirt that hung open in front and white sandals on her feet. Sunlight washed through the lobby and seemed to practically glow as it gilded Julie. She looked fresh and beautiful and his body stirred hard and hot right there in the hotel lobby.

Damned if he could figure out just why she affected him as she did, but as long as they were married, he planned to make the most of it. Before he could reach out and cup her cheek, though, a voice sounded from behind him.

"Travis, I am sorry to see you go so soon."

Turning, he held out one hand. "Rico, your timing, as always, sucks."

His cousin laughed as if he knew exactly what Travis meant.

"But we appreciate the hospitality," Travis said.

"Yes," Julie added. "Thank you. Your hotel is just gorgeous and we had a—" she sent Travis a small smile "—wonderful time."

They had, Travis mused, watching her luscious mouth curve. Except for the paparazzi and the delays in the divorce and the minor crisis of photos taken at a private moment ending up on the front page of national newspapers. But she was standing there smiling, her green eyes shining, as if they hadn't had any trouble at all.

He was forced to admit that Julie had taken all of this mess in stride. Much better than any other woman he knew would have done. Hell, if it weren't for her even keel and stubborn calm, he probably would have gone over the edge himself.

Not a happy thought, he told himself. He didn't like the fact that he'd needed her to keep him calm. And thinking of that, why the hell *had* she been relatively calm about all of this? Was she really so damned easygoing? Or was it that she'd known ahead of time about all the problems that would arise because she'd been in on planning them from the start?

Hell, he hadn't *planned* to seduce her on the damn balcony. But she'd looked so blasted edible, he hadn't been able to help himself. Had she seduced him? Arranged for a photographer to catch them at an inopportune moment? But why? Hell, she'd been even more embarrassed and angry than he had. At least, he told himself, she'd seemed to be. And what about Jean Claude? How the devil had that little weasel managed to get onto the winery property on a day when Travis had had extra security measures in place? Had Julie helped him sneak past the guards?

And what about their first night of amazing—*unprotected*—sex? Why the *hell* hadn't she been on the Pill? Had she actually been trying to get pregnant and hold him up for more cash?

"Travis?" Her voice prodded at him and her

tone said she'd already called his name a couple of times. "Earth to Travis…."

"What?" He came up out of his thoughts with a dark scowl on his face and suspicion crawling through his system.

She shook her head as she watched him. "Are you feeling okay?"

"Fine." The word was bitten off as he struggled to get past the misgivings still simmering inside him. "Why?"

"You must forgive him," Rico said with a laugh. "A freshly wed man has many things on his mind."

She looked as though she didn't believe that excuse, but at the moment, Travis didn't really care if she bought it or not. He just wanted to get moving. Get back to California and the winery. If Julie really were in cahoots with Jean Claude, Travis would discover the truth sooner once he was back on his own home turf.

"You are most welcome here anytime, Julie." Rico's accent flowed musically across his words as he took her hand, turned it over and kissed her knuckles.

Travis shot his new wife a look to see her reaction and damned if she didn't look charmed.

"Oh, please," Travis muttered, glaring at the other man.

"Forgive my cousin," Rico said, smiling. "He has no appreciation for the finer things in life."

"Okay," Travis interrupted, unamused by his cousin. "We'd better get a move on."

But just then, a young woman in a hotel uniform hurried up to Rico's side, and tapped his arm to get his attention.

"Pardon, Señor King," she said and when he turned to her, she leaned in close and whispered something neither Julie or Travis could quite catch.

While they waited, Travis looked at Julie, bent his head so that his low-pitched voice was heard by her alone and asked, "Impressed by Rico, are you?"

Julie grinned up at him and something inside Travis fisted at the brightness of her eyes and the flush on her cheeks.

"He's gorgeous, and he kissed my hand," she said. "Who wouldn't be impressed?"

Travis stared into her eyes. "Just remember which King you're married to."

"Hmm…" She tipped her head to one side and pretended to have to think about that one for a second.

"Having trouble?" he asked, not liking the stir of something like possessiveness that rose up inside him. Temporary wife or not, Julie was his for the next year and he didn't want her forgetting that for a second. "Let me refresh your memory."

Heedless of the smattering of hotel guests wandering through the lobby, Travis grabbed her, pulled her up close and kissed her hard, long and deep. Every cell in his body sent up a shout of exaltation and even while he was tasting her, he knew it wouldn't be enough.

For good or bad, she'd gotten into his blood in the last week or two. He wanted her every damn minute. Something he hadn't expected. Hadn't been looking for. And, since he couldn't very well do what he wanted to do to her in the middle of a hotel lobby, he broke their kiss, straightened up and set her back on her feet.

"Wow," she whispered, lifting one hand to her mouth as she swayed unsteadily.

He smiled, enjoying the knowledge that she was as affected as he. "Better than a kiss on the knuckles?"

She licked her lips and sent an arrow of heat darting straight through him. "Yeah. Way better."

Julie felt warm all over, a deliciously wicked sensation she'd become all too familiar with in the last couple of weeks. One touch of

Travis's hand, or a single kiss, was enough to make her blood sizzle with need.

Since their little "talk" in the park a few days ago, he hadn't once even hinted that he actually thought she'd tried to get pregnant on purpose. Did that mean he believed her? Or was he simply better at hiding his feelings than she was?

In fact, they hadn't discussed that wild, unprotected first night together at all. It was as if each of them were trying to pretend it had never happened. And maybe that was best. Because if she thought about it too much, she'd make herself insane.

Beside her, Travis hooked one arm around her waist and pulled her in close. His body heat reached for her even as a whisper of cool air swept across Julie's shoulders, making her shiver a bit. It wasn't a foreboding of anything, she told herself, just the excellent hotel air conditioner. But as Rico continued a whispered conversation with his employee and Julie saw the man's expression shift from charming to thunderous, she braced herself.

Ever since they'd arranged for the divorce and the remarriage, things had been better between her and Travis and she was really hoping that whatever crisis had Rico looking so concerned had nothing to do with *them*. She actually felt as though she and her brand-new, temporary husband had reached a sort of détente.

They weren't exactly a real team, but they were vaguely on the same side. Sure, Travis was still bossy and arrogant and too darn sure of himself all the time, with a real tendency to try to put her in a corner and make her stay there...but that she could handle. It was the outside problems that were making her crazy.

"Something's wrong," Travis finally said, looking at his cousin.

"I know," Julie whispered, and wondered

now if that blast of air-conditioned air hadn't been more than a stray chill after all.

Rico turned to them as his employee scuttled away. His dark features were tight and furious, his black eyes snapping with indignation. Drawing the two of them to one side, he glanced briefly at Julie then turned his gaze on Travis. "There's trouble."

"Damn it," Travis muttered and his arm around her waist tightened reflexively. "What is it now?"

"Someone in the judge's office has leaked the news of Julie's divorce and your secretive marriage to the press." Rico shifted his dark eyes from Travis to Julie and back again.

"How? What? The *press?*" The relief Julie had felt only moments ago was gone as if it had never existed. Instead, there was a cold, hard knot of worry settling in the pit of her stomach. What else could possibly go wrong?

Rico spared her a sympathetic glance, but

Travis was clearly too busy steaming to worry about how she was feeling. Fury literally radiated off his body until Julie wouldn't have been surprised to see ripples of heat waves rolling across the hotel lobby. She couldn't really blame him. She, too, was reeling from this latest jolt.

How could she possibly have gone her whole life being pretty much invisible to the world and have that all change in less than two weeks?

"How much does the press know?" Travis demanded.

"Everything," Rico told him, keeping his voice low. "The story broke early this morning. Should be all over the wire services by now. The idiot law clerk kept nothing to himself. It is small consolation I know—" he added with sympathy "—but Judge Hernandez has already fired the man."

"You're right. That is small consolation."

Shoving a hand through his hair, Travis gritted his teeth and looked as if he wanted to kick something. "This is just great. We went through all of this for nothing."

"It would seem so," Rico said.

Julie couldn't believe it. It was like a bad dream that was stuck on rewind. Now, because of one man's greed, she and Travis had been exposed to the press. Again. But this was far worse than an embarrassing photograph. This was digging into their lives, exposing secrets. This wasn't just her breasts displayed for public consumption.

This was her *life*.

Looking up at Travis, she wondered if he was sorry now that he'd come to her with this little bargain. Of course he was. And why wouldn't he be? Ever since they'd walked down the aisle together, there'd been nothing but one disaster after another. How could he *not* wish her to the other side of the earth?

"If I ever get my hands on that law clerk," Travis muttered.

"He is no doubt long gone already," Rico said just as tightly. "Probably counting his money."

Julie didn't care where the little worm was. She just wanted to know what they were supposed to do next. She wanted to know that Travis and she were still in this together. Would he stick with her? Honor their bargain? Or would he want to dissolve this mess before anything else happened?

She really hoped not. Because if he walked away from their oh-so-new marriage right now, she'd be all alone facing a rabid media.

"Travis?" Julie finally found her voice and when she spoke, she captured his attention. "What happens now?"

Features tight, dark eyes glinting with an anger that colored his voice, he didn't even look at her as he simply said, "We go home."

"*We?*"

One dark eyebrow lifted as he turned a hard look on her. "You'd rather go alone?"

"No," she said quickly. God, no. "I just didn't—"

"We're married, aren't we?" he asked, giving her a smile that went nowhere near his eyes.

"Yes, we are," she said, returning that cold smile with one of her own. They were married and even though it looked as though they were going to stay that way, at least for now, Julie felt a yawning distance open up between them.

And she didn't have a single idea how to close it.

Rico had been right, of course. The minute the King jet landed at a private airstrip near Birkfield, reporters had crowded around Travis and Julie like jackals after a particularly tasty corpse.

And as ugly as that analogy was, it hadn't gotten any better over the last week.

Leaning back in his desk chair, Travis clutched the telephone to his ear and listened distractedly to the Muzak especially designed to drive a man insane. He didn't have the option of hanging up in frustration though. He had to talk to Thomas Henry and the man had been avoiding his calls for days now.

This time, Travis was determined to reach him.

Scowling, he sent a distracted glance around his study. The walls were a deep, dark red, and white crown molding ran around the circumference of the room just below the ceiling. Bookcases studded the walls along with paintings Travis had commissioned of the vineyards. He'd always seen this room as a sort of sanctuary. He locked himself in here to work and frequently sat in one of the oversized, black leather chairs to relax in front of the fire.

Today, though, relaxing wasn't on the agenda.

"I'm sorry, Mr. King." The elevator music stopped abruptly as a woman's voice came over the line. "But Mr. Henry is still busy. Are you sure you want to hold? I can give him a message and ask him to return your call."

Busy. Travis didn't believe that for a second. Henry was dodging him. Damned successfully so far, too. Strange, but Travis had gotten married to *improve* his chances at a distribution deal. And yet, ever since he'd walked down the aisle with Julie, that elusive deal had drifted further and further out of reach.

Well, nobody stalled a King for long. And he'd be damned if he'd leave yet another message for Henry. Travis had already tried that approach twice. This time, he'd stay on the phone until the damn thing became attached to his ear if he had to. He didn't give in, never surrendered, and Thomas Henry would damn well talk to him whether the man wanted to or not.

"Thanks," he said, keeping his voice politely neutral. "I'll hold."

She sighed. "Very well."

Instantly, the music was back and Travis was left with his own thoughts again. Not the most pleasant alternative lately. He and Julie had settled into a routine of sorts, but the easy camaraderie they'd experienced in Mexico had disappeared.

Granted, he hadn't been the most approachable person over the last week. But Julie'd been just as distracted. What with reporters haunting their every step and the phone ringing nonstop, she was so on edge she jumped whenever he walked into the room. A part of him wanted to hold her, bury himself inside her and tuck the problems surrounding them into the background. But he couldn't do that while another part of him still wondered if she wasn't somehow involved in all of this.

Talking to his brothers hadn't helped any.

He stared at the far wall, gaze fixed on a painting of the winery, but he wasn't seeing the crisp colors or the subtle brush strokes. Instead, he thought back to the conversation he'd had with his brothers the night before.

"Our lawyers are working on Julie's ex," Adam had said.

"Can't we have him arrested for something?" Jackson wanted to know.

"He hasn't done anything illegal," Travis responded. "Yet."

Adam reminded him, "He blackmailed you."

"Fine. He did. And if I admit to that, it's just one more piece of news for the press," Travis replied. "No thanks. I already feel like there are photographers hiding in the vines. I don't need more of the same."

"This mess is just getting worse." Adam said.

"Really? Hadn't noticed." Travis's wry tone seemed to irritate Adam further. "I asked you to look in to the guy's past. Didn't you find anything we can use to make him disappear?"

"No." Adam said. "As far as we can tell, he's never tried blackmail before."

"Pity," Jackson commented. "Since he seems to have a flair for it."

"There's got to be something. He's playing this in the press as though he's a wounded, discarded lover."

"What does Julie have to say about all of this anyway?" Adam asked.

"What do you think she's got to say?" Travis demanded softly. "She's embarrassed and pissed off, just like me."

"Is she?" Jackson asked quietly.

Travis stared at his younger brother and fought down the anger that seemed to have become a permanent part of him. "What's that supposed to mean?"

"Don't get me wrong, I like Julie. A lot. I'm just thinking that all hell's broken loose since you two decided to get married."

"It is an interesting question," Adam pointed out.

"You, too?" Travis had asked his older brother.

"Can you say you're absolutely positive that Julie's innocent?"

Could he? No. Was he going to admit that to his brothers and have to listen to their opinions? No. He ran his own life. And he'd deal with his marriage himself. He didn't need a committee.

"Yeah," he lied. "I can."

Adam watched him for a long minute or two, before finally nodding. "All right then. That's good enough for me. You and Julie keep a low profile, for God's sake. All of this press attention is making Gina a nervous wreck and she doesn't need that with the baby due any day."

"It's not like I'm enjoying the media circus myself, you know."

Adam ignored that. "Jackson and I will keep looking for information on Jean Claude. There's bound to be something somewhere in his background."

"Yeah," Jackson said. "Maybe we can find a reporter to work for us for a change. Maybe hint that Jean Claude's not all he seems to be."

"Worth a shot," Travis said.

And it was worth looking in to, he thought as he came out of the memory like a man who'd been asleep too long and couldn't quite shake the cobwebs out of his mind.

The only thing that concerned him was if they did find something on Jean Claude, would the information implicate Julie, as well? He didn't want to think so. Not only because it would be infuriating as hell to be so completely wrong about a person but also because he'd have to live with her duplicity for the next year. He'd be damned if he'd enter into another media feeding frenzy that would ensue if he tried for a quick divorce from her.

Travis shook his head and shoved one hand through his hair. Fisting his hand around the damn phone that continued to spew hideous music into his ear, he fought down the urge to throw the phone across the room. He might not be able to straighten out one part of his life, but he for damn sure was going to iron out a deal with Thomas Henry or die trying.

"King?" A deep, brusque voice interrupted Travis's thoughts. "What is it?"

"Henry," Travis said, sitting up straight in his chair, keeping his voice pleasantly, deliberately even. "I've been trying to reach you."

"Been busy," the other man said.

"Right. Me, too." Travis knew the older man had been reading the newspapers, following the scandal that had risen up around Travis and

Julie, so the first order of business was to smooth that over. "I've been dealing with lawyers for the last week. Not the way I'd planned on spending the first weeks of my marriage."

"Yes," Henry mused. "I've been reading about you and your wife."

"I can imagine," Travis said. "But I want to assure you that there is no truth to the stories you've been seeing in the press about us."

"So she wasn't married to this...Doucette character?"

Scowling, Travis picked up a pen from the top of his desk, tapped it on the oak surface, then tossed it aside again. "Actually, yes, she was."

"Well, then—you're both getting exactly what she deserves," the man blustered, a dismissive tone in his voice that sent a blast of protective fury whipping through Travis.

"Doucette tricked my wife," he said, voice hard. Yeah, he wanted the distribution contract, but he'd be damned if he'd sit here and let someone who didn't even know her insult Julie. "She's done nothing wrong and I don't appreciate your innuendo."

"Now just one minute…"

"No, Henry," Travis said, standing up as he allowed his anger to swell inside him. "You wait a minute. It's true I want your company to distribute my wine, but I can live without it." He didn't want to. Hadn't planned to. But he wasn't going to sit back and let someone stomp on him, either.

It wouldn't be easy to find a good distributor if this deal didn't come through, but he'd find a way and damned if Travis King was going to kiss anyone's ass just to move along the success train. "You know as well as I do that a deal with King wines would serve you as well as me."

"Who do you think you're talking to?"

"I could ask the same, Henry," Travis said and shoved one hand into the pocket of his slacks. His voice was deep and dark and filled with the venom that was coursing through his veins. "I'm not some green kid just breaking in to the wine business. I've got one of the top wineries in California and you know it. King wines is growing every year. Now we can work together to build the name into something that will make us both a lot of money—" he paused, took a breath and tamped down the anger nearly choking him "—or you can utter one more insult toward my wife and I hang up and find a new distributor."

For one split second, Travis wondered if he'd gone too far—if the other man was going to hang up and forget about King wineries. Then that moment passed and the other man spoke up again.

"You're right," Henry said thoughtfully. "And I admire a man who stands for his family. I'm willing to discuss the distribution deal. Let's meet next week to talk it over."

Success. It tasted bittersweet, but Travis could choke it down. When he hung up, Travis thought about going to tell Julie the good news. Then he reconsidered. After all, it wasn't as if this was a *real* marriage.

Upstairs, Julie closed the door to the master bedroom, stepped over to the wide window that overlooked the acres of neatly tended grape vines. White, billowy clouds drifted like sails across a sky so blue it almost hurt to look at it. Sunlight slanted down on the vineyard and just for a moment, Julie took a breath and paused simply to enjoy the beauty of the scene.

But she hadn't come upstairs to admire the King winery. She'd come for a little privacy. She wasn't going to be a passive observer in her life anymore. It was time that Julie faced her past and did something about straightening out her future. Flipping open her cell phone, she dialed a number she'd tried to forget. Waiting impatiently as the phone rang, she tugged at the white sheers hanging alongside the window and almost jumped when a man's voice came on the line.

"Hello?"

God, how she hated that voice.

"Jean Claude," she said. "We have to talk."

Eight

Julie felt like a spy.

Any minute now, she half expected Travis to jump out from the shadows, point an accusing finger at her and shout *Traitor!*

"This was probably a bad idea," she muttered and carried her hot cup of coffee to the scratched-up white guardrail at the edge of the lookout over the ocean. She hunched a little deeper into her dark blue windbreaker and turned her face into the wind, letting that icy breeze blow her hair back from her face.

She was alone on the wide, half moon of asphalt, her car the only one parked on the turnout some twenty miles north of the King winery. Highway 1 traveled up the length of California, going through tiny towns, and winding along the rugged coastline. Up and down the state there were wide pullouts just like this one, where tourists could stop, park the car and take photos of the incredible scenery.

Ordinarily, Julie would be just as caught up in the beauty of the place as anyone else. But today, all she saw were the gathering dark clouds on the horizon and the never ending stretch of steel-gray sea. It was as if the whole world were suddenly in black and white. And she knew that's how Travis would see this little meeting of hers. Black and white.

Friend and enemy.

If he discovered that she'd come to meet Jean Claude of her own accord… "Oh, don't even go there, Julie," she told herself, backing away from that thought as she would have from a rabid dog.

She deliberately kept her face turned away from the highway and the forest. For all she knew, there might be reporters and photographers out there, aiming their telephoto lenses and parabolic microphones directly at her. Not that she was paranoid or anything, but over the last two weeks, she'd been dissected for public consumption almost every day.

Which is why she'd asked Jean Claude to meet her here. Even if it was a stupid maneuver, at least she felt as though she was doing *something* to try to stop all of this.

A car pulled up beside hers and Julie stiffened as she turned to watch Jean Claude park his spiffy, two-seater sports car. He climbed out lazily, a man completely at ease. His blond hair lifted from his forehead and Julie absently noted that it looked thinner than she remembered.

"New car?" she asked. A splashy one, too.

Leave it to Jean Claude, to whom appearances meant more than anything else. He used to love talking about his grandfather, who had been a minor member of the aristocracy. No doubt, Jean Claude was just loving being the center of a media storm. Everyone wanted to talk to him. Tabloids and TV stations were willing to pay him to smile on camera and dish out dirt that made him look like a forgotten lover.

All he'd had to do was sell her out and make her and Travis's lives a living hell. Julie's insides twisted as she watched him shoot a loving glance at the sports car.

He trailed one finger along the shining red hood. "Yes, lovely little thing, isn't it?"

Obviously, Jean Claude was enjoying the money he'd made both from the blackmail and the constant streams of interviews he'd given.

He walked toward her, a smile on the face she'd once thought so handsome. "Julie, *ma chérie,* what a delight it is to see you."

She backed up, keeping a safe distance between them. She didn't think she'd be able to stand it if he got close enough to touch her. How could she ever have convinced herself she loved this man enough to marry him? She was *such* an idiot.

He smiled again as if he knew what she was thinking. God, was she doing the right thing by setting up this meeting? Would this only make things worse? If Travis found out about this—

"Jean Claude—"

"This is very sexy, no?" He glanced around at the empty area, then shifted his gaze back to her. "Just the two of us. All alone."

She only *hoped* they were alone and that there were no reporters or photographers hiding somewhere nearby.

"No," she said with a firm shake of her head. "I mean, yes, we're alone, but no, it's not sexy."

The wind whipped his blond hair back from

his forehead, displaying a lot *more* forehead than she remembered. Apparently being a full-time jerk caused premature balding. Small consolation.

"Fine," he said with a shrug. "If you do not wish to enjoy a clandestine tryst, why did you want to meet?"

"A tryst?" Her mouth dropped open. "Are you insane?"

"Do you not remember how it once was between us, *chérie?*" His voice was low, and what he no doubt considered his "seductive" tone.

But when Julie thought back on her time with this man and then compared it to the nights spent in Travis's bed, the differences were nearly laughable. Jean Claude thought a lot more of himself than he had a right to.

Obviously, he read her expression clearly because he shrugged again and said, "Fine, then. Tell me what you want from me."

"I want you to stop what you're doing to me and Travis."

"Stop?" His eyebrows lifted and a smile pulled at one corner of his mouth. "Why would I want to do that?"

"Haven't you done enough, Jean Claude?" she asked, taking a step toward him before stopping again. "Haven't you made enough money off of embarrassing Travis and I?"

He straightened. "No. I believe there is much more to be had and I am not finished."

Her stomach felt as if an invisible someone had dropped a cold rock into it. She had known going into this meeting that he would fight her on this, but she had had to try.

"Jean Claude, you're ruining a man who doesn't deserve this. And I'm not going to let you."

"How will you stop me?"

"I'll go to the police. Travis won't, he wants to handle this himself. But I'll have you arrested. For blackmail."

He smiled at her and clucked his tongue. *"Chérie..."*

"Stop saying that!" She walked even closer, poked him in the chest with her index finger. "Back off now, Jean Claude."

"Why should I?" he interrupted with a laugh.

"I'm not the foolish woman who once married you. I'm willing to see you in jail, or deported."

"You wouldn't. Besides you have no proof."

"I can get it. Don't push me on this."

"I don't believe you." Then he bent his head and kissed her before she could jump out of the way.

Wiping one hand across her mouth as if she'd been poisoned, Julie stumbled backward, her gaze fixed on his. "You stay away from me, Jean Claude. And you back off of Travis before you end up behind bars."

"Is that a threat?" He laughed and folded his arms over his chest. "Perhaps I should alert the papers that now Travis King is threatening me—the poor, set-aside lover."

"Travis didn't threaten you, Jean Claude. *I* did." She glared at him and it only irritated her further that he didn't look the least bit worried. "Blackmail is a crime, Jean Claude."

"Ah," he said, smiling and perfectly at ease. "Bigamy is also a crime, *ma chérie*. Do you really wish to meet me in a court of law?"

What Julie really wanted was to strangle him, but unfortunately, that was a crime, too. Though she was willing to bet that a jury of women would exonerate her. She could just kick herself for ever setting up this meeting. She'd so hoped she could somehow end this lingering nightmare. Now all she wanted was to get as far away from this man as she possibly could. She stalked across the lot to her car and when she opened the driver's side door, she stopped and looked back at him.

"Don't push me, Jean Claude. Take what you have and disappear. Leave us alone."

"I will see you soon," he called back and gave her a wave.

When she left, spinning her wheels on the asphalt, Julie looked into her rearview mirror and saw Jean Claude on his cell phone.

Probably not a good sign.

Two hours later, Travis jumped down from the driver's side of his truck and slammed the door behind him. The sun was hot, but the breeze was cool. Not cool enough to take the edge off the fury currently burning his insides like a brushfire out of control, though.

Seemed he'd been angry ever since he'd come up with the insane idea of getting married. And there was no end in sight. Now he was getting phone calls from a Realtor about his "wife" looking for property she hadn't bothered to talk to him about.

He didn't see her car, but Main Street was crowded. She could be parked just about anywhere. Birkfield was small, but bustling. Local residents usually did their shopping here, rather than take the freeway into one of the bigger cities more than an hour away. Plus, the town got a good share of tourist business as well, with people driving up the coast and stopping for a little break at the many wineries nearby.

Main Street was filled with antique stores, specialty shops, restaurants and the kinds of stores small communities all required. Hardware, groceries, post office—all crowded together on both sides of the two-lane street. Birkfield was small, true, but Travis had always loved that about the place.

At least, until recently. Now there were way too many people who felt as though they had a proprietary interest in his life. And thanks to the newspapers, tabloids and weekly trashy magazines, there was plenty of fodder to feed the local gossips.

Just what he needed.

"Afternoon, Travis," a familiar voice called from the sidewalk in front of the local hardware store.

He muffled a groan, turned and forced a smile. Speak of the gossip. "Mrs. James. How are you?"

"Fine, fine. Been real exciting around here lately, thanks to you and Julie."

"Yeah." Too exciting. Just standing here, he felt as though he were under a microscope. His friends and neighbors, people he'd grown up around, people he'd known his whole life, were now watching him with avid interest.

Funny, all the times he'd gotten his picture in the paper by dating some model or actress had never gotten him the kind of attention marrying a hometown girl/bigamist had.

The older woman shook her head and gave

a cluck of her tongue. "But then, you knew Julie was a caution even before you married her, now didn't you?"

He didn't get a chance to answer because the woman who had once been his fifth grade teacher just rolled right on.

"Of course, as I recall, you two used to be thick as thieves when you were children." She tipped her head back and studied the sky. "I told that nice young reporter about the time I had to chase you two out of the janitor's closet. Of course, you were both just kids then, but Julie was so sweet on you—though it was inappropriate, of course."

He'd been nodding along, just to hurry the woman up until that last sentence caught his attention. "Inappropriate?"

"Well, you know. With her mother being your family's cook and all."

Travis just stared at her. He couldn't think of anything to say that wouldn't come out rude, so he decided it was best to just keep nodding and move along. Still, it amazed him the things people came up with.

Inappropriate? "Good seeing you, Mrs. James."

He hadn't taken more than a step when she called out, "Are you looking for Julie?"

Closing his eyes, Travis took a deep breath and said pleasantly, "Yes, I am. Do you know where she is?"

"I should say so. Didn't I see her only five minutes ago, down at the old tavern?" She clucked her tongue again in displeasure. "They ought to tear that eyesore down is what they ought to do, but does the town council listen to me?"

He sympathized with the town council.

"Thanks." He shoved one hand through his hair, nodded to Mrs. James and turned for the far side of the street.

He did a lazy run across the two lanes of

traffic, lifting one hand to the cars who stopped to let him pass. At the far end of the street, he spotted a news van and hoped they hadn't spotted him. He would have thought there would be something more interesting than his life happening somewhere. But no, reporters and photographers were still dotting the streets of Birkfield, waiting for the latest installment in the King drama.

Travis kept his gaze focused straight ahead of him as he darted in and out of strolling pedestrians on his walk up the sidewalk. The scent of something delicious wafted out of the diner and his stomach grumbled in response. He'd been out working the vines all morning with his crew, just to get away from the damned phones, and his hunger marched in time with his anger.

The long-vacated bar stood between a candle shop and an art gallery featuring the work of local artists. The wide front window was covered in grime, but the door was unlocked. Travis threw a glance over his shoulder, opened the door and stepped into the dimness.

Almost no sunlight at all made it through that front window and the overhead light boasted one low-wattage bulb. Shadows clung to the walls and hid behind stacked boxes left behind by the last tenant. There was no sign of life here, but Travis could sense Julie's presence. He didn't even want to think about why that was.

"Julie?"

"Back here!" Her voice sounded muffled and he cursed under his breath as he walked toward it. What the hell was she up to, anyway?

He stepped through another open door into what must have passed for the kitchen, only to spot Julie, on her knees, sticking her head into an oven that looked older than him. "What're you doing here?"

She backed out, turned her face up to his and grinned, oblivious to the streak of dirt across her nose. "A better question, how'd you know where to find me?"

He stuffed his hands into his jeans pockets and took the few steps separating them. "I got a call from Donna Vega. She tells me you're interested in the property."

Her grin slipped a little, but she clambered to her feet and looked around the dingy, dirty room with a gleam in her eye before she turned back to him. "I didn't think she'd call you. I was going to tell you myself later—"

"Tell me what exactly?"

She brushed her hands together in a futile attempt to dislodge the black streaks covering her palms. "I was out driving and saw the for sale sign in the window, so I stopped to take a look. I called Donna to let me in so I could explore a little."

"That explains what you're doing. Not why."

She whipped her short, curly hair off her face with a toss of her head. "I'm going to be opening a bakery, in about a year, remember? This place would be perfect."

He shook his head. "This place is only suitable for firewood."

"You have no imagination."

Travis tried to see what she did in the old bar, but frankly, it escaped him. But that wasn't the point right now anyway. "You shouldn't be doing this now."

"What?"

"Looking at property," he said with a wave of his hand to indicate the decrepit building. "Haven't we got enough to deal with at the moment?"

"Travis," she said, looking into his eyes. "This has nothing to do with any of the other stuff going on."

"No?" He cocked his head, folded his arms across his chest and tried not to breathe. There was a very weird smell in the room. "You don't think the reporters following us around would love to print the story of King's new wife going out to open her own business? King wives don't have to work."

"What planet are you from?" Julie demanded, hands at her hips and feet braced for battle.

"Just a minute—"

"No, you wait a minute." She tipped her head to one side as if she were thinking deeply, then said, "I suppose you don't remember your mom doing ranch work every day."

"That was different," Travis argued.

"It was work. Work she loved doing," Julie shot right back.

"My mom is not the point here."

"No, she's not," Julie said. "But Gina is a 'King wife' and *she* works. She raises and trains horses."

"At the home ranch."

"Oh, so it's not the work that bothers you, it's *where* your wife works?"

Was it completely crazy, Travis wondered, that he liked that fire in her eyes? Probably.

"Not the point," he said tightly. "You're not opening the bakery until *after* the marriage is over, so why get people talking now? Don't we have enough going on at the moment anyway? Damn it, Julie, we're supposed to be a united front. How's it look to everyone if you're sneaking around behind my back?"

She flushed and her gaze shifted to one side. Her mouth went firm and tight and she rocked uneasily on her heels. "I hate it when you're right."

"That was too easy," he muttered, wondering what else was going on in her mind. It wasn't like her to give up so quickly.

"Well, I wasn't thinking how it would look to everyone else in town. And I hate having to worry about how something looks to somebody else. Why should they care what we do? Why are we big news?"

"Hell if I know," Travis said. "Maybe people don't have enough excitement in their own lives so they need to find it somewhere else."

"Does it have to be *us?*"

"At the moment," he conceded, hating it every bit as much as she did. "Sooner or later though, some other poor fool will get into the spotlight and we'll fade away. Until then…"

She lifted her gaze to his again. "I know, I know. I wasn't sneaking, Travis. I saw the place and stopped for a look. I was going to tell you. I mean, if I'm going to tell you something, that can't be sneaky by definition, right?"

"Uh-huh." He was getting a fairly uneasy feeling about all this now. "What else don't I know?"

Nine

"**Y**ou didn't mention the fact that you *kissed* him!"

Travis's voice echoed off the high ceiling in the tasting room at the winery. The gleaming oak-paneled room was empty but for the two of them and for a moment, Julie really wished for the crowd that was due to arrive at any moment.

Twice a week, the King winery hosted tastings in this room. Busloads of tourists wandered through this room, the winemaking area and the gift shop. They tasted wine, snacked on the offerings that Julie herself made for the occasions and, in general, had a lovely time while providing a nice distraction for everyone else from the everyday work of the winery.

She looked up from the elegant table set with china, old silver and the appetizers and desserts she'd spent most of the day cooking. There were tiny, perfect shrimp, dark green sprigs of prosciutto-wrapped asparagus and gourmet crackers dotted with a feta/spinach mixture. The desserts were nearby and looking just as tempting—lemon tarts, brownie bits with hot fudge baked inside and tiny shortbread cookies dipped in an almond cream sauce. And yes, she was thinking about food because she wasn't quite ready to concentrate on her husband just yet.

Hopefully, the finger foods she'd spent hours putting together would entice their visitors far more than they interested her at the moment.

But then, the strangers headed for the winery wouldn't be facing the thundercloud of Travis's expression. Julie's stomach churned uneasily and she swallowed hard to avoid the sudden rush of nausea filling her mouth.

Watching as Travis stalked across the shining wood floor, she nearly groaned at the flash of fury in his eyes. Apparently, she wasn't going to be feeling better anytime soon. The way he shook the newspaper he held told her that she wasn't going to like what was in it.

A sinking sensation opened up inside her and she really wished she could avoid this confrontation. She didn't much care if that made her a coward or not.

Yesterday, she'd confessed to her meeting with Jean Claude and had thought that after that explosive argument with Travis, the subject would be buried. Naturally, her life just wasn't that easy.

And how strange was it that even facing Travis when he was angry, she felt a rush of heat that pushed through her bloodstream in a frantic race. He wore an expensively cut black suit, white dress shirt and a bold red tie. His dark hair was ruffled and his eyes were flashing.

The man was gorgeous. Even when he looked as though he could bite through a steel bar.

When he reached the table she stood behind, he stopped directly opposite her and shook the newspaper again in one tight fist. "When you told me about your little meeting with *Pierre,*" he growled. "You neglected to tell me just how cozy it was."

"It wasn't cozy," she argued, making a grab for the paper. He snatched it back and she stared directly into his eyes, giving back as good as she got. Fine, he was mad. Well, join the club. She was more than tired of being dragged through public scrutiny by a scandal-hungry press. And defending herself to the one man who should have a little faith in her was getting to be just as irritating. "If you think I would willingly kiss that little worm, you're nuts."

"A picture's worth ten thousand words," he said, and held the paper up in front of him, showing her the front page.

"Oh, God."

There it was. In startlingly clear black and white. A picture of the moment when Jean Claude had bent down to touch his thin, nasty lips to hers. Apparently, he *had* had a photographer stationed somewhere nearby. She never should have tried reasoning with a man who had no morals. This was her fault. All of it.

"He was probably hiding in the trees," she muttered.

"Who?"

"The photographer, of course!" She grabbed at the paper again, but Travis shook his head, turned it in his hands and read the words beneath the photo aloud instead.

"Clandestine lovers?"

Shock had her jaw dropping. "Cland—"

"Jean Claude Doucette and Julie O'Hara Doucette King—"

Appalled, Julie screwed up her mouth as if she'd bitten into a lemon. "I don't still have his name, do I?"

"Meet secretly at a lookout on Highway One."

"That sounds horrible…."

His gaze lifted to hers and in those dark brown depths, she could have sworn she saw actual *flames*. "Oh, it gets better," he assured her. "The story that accompanies the picture wonders if Travis King knows that his wife is still in love with the man she never bothered to divorce before moving on to another marriage."

Now his eyes were dark, unfathomable. His jaw was clenched and his mouth was hardly more than a slash across his face. Even though he was standing directly opposite her, she felt as closed off from him as if she'd been in a sealed room.

And still, she had to say, "Travis, you can't believe that."

"What do you expect me to believe," he whispered angrily. "You set up a meeting with him."

"Yes," she said, lifting her index finger to make the point. "But I told you about it afterward."

His eyes fixed on hers and Julie felt the hard slam of his silent accusation just seconds before he said it aloud.

"You should have told me *before* you did it, so there would have been time to stop you."

She sighed a little, anger blending with frustration and sorrow. "That's why I didn't."

"Why the hell did you go to see him? What was so damned important you had to go behind my back and meet up with your ex-husband?"

"I explained this yesterday, Travis," she

said, forcing patience into her being, though she actually felt like jumping up and down and tearing at her hair. He had to have the hardest head she'd ever come up against. "It was something I had to do. I had to try to reason with Jean Claude myself."

"I've got lawyers I'm paying to stop him. My brothers are looking in to it."

Frustration bubbled into a froth inside her, swamping her sorrow, drowning even the anger. "You just don't get it, Travis. I'm not the stay-at-home, wait-for-the-big-brave-man-to-take-care-of-things kind of woman." She pushed her hands through her hair then let them drop to her sides again. "Don't you see? Jean Claude is bothering you because of *me*. He's only giving you this much trouble because I was once stupid enough to marry him. It was up to *me* to face him."

"Damn it, Julie." He crumpled the paper in his fist and squeezed.

"I had to do something, Travis," she said, her voice getting stronger with every word. "I take care of myself. I always have. I don't know how to do anything else and frankly, I wouldn't want to. This whole mess was, at the heart of it, my fault. So it was up to me to fix it."

"You did a hell of a job," he said, shaking the wadded-up newspaper again.

"Yeah, well…" Her frustration bubbled a little hotter, a little thicker. "I gave it a shot. Something I had to do. I just should have remembered that I was dealing with a snake. No," she corrected herself quickly. "Something that crawls *under* snakes. Or maybe something that snakes ooze through."

"He kissed you." The words were soft, barely audible, and she watched as an emotion she'd never seen before shot across his eyes and disappeared again a moment later.

What was it? What was he feeling? Was it

only anger? Or was there something more? Something deeper?

Grumbling, she admitted, "He moves pretty fast for a snake."

Travis came around the table, smoothed her hair back from her face, then cupped the back of her neck with his big palm. "I didn't like seeing him touching you."

Her heartbeat quickened and her blood felt hot and thick in her veins. One touch from this man and she was butter on a stove. "Trust me, I didn't like it much, either."

"I want to," he said.

"What?" God, she could hardly think with his hand on her.

"Trust you. I want to trust you, Julie."

Everything in her went still as glass. She looked up into his eyes and felt the threads of connection stretching between them. Could he feel it? Did he ache for her touch as she did for his? Did his skin sizzle from the contact of hers? Did he feel more than he'd wanted or expected to?

Could he see in her eyes that she loved him?

She loved him.

Julie swayed a little as that acknowledgement sank in. She had loved him almost from the start, she knew that now. Or maybe she'd always loved him and had somehow buried that knowledge deep inside. All she could be sure of was that since their wedding night, her heart had been his.

If only he wanted it.

"You can trust me, Travis."

He smiled a little, no more than a slight curving of his mouth, but it briefly lightened the darkness of his eyes. Then he moved his hand, stroked her cheek with the tips of his fingers and dropped his palm to her bare shoulder. Where their flesh met, there was heat. Electricity. And a sense of pulse-pounding urgency that told her she wanted him now. Wanted his body covering hers. Wanted to feel that intimate slide of bodies meshing, becoming one. Wanted to luxuriate in the sensations that she could only find with Travis.

But this wasn't the time. Or the place. Even as he touched her, she felt the reserve in him. As if he were holding himself back from her deliberately.

"Trust isn't something that comes easy to me, Julie."

"Try, Travis," she urged. "You've known me most of my life and I think somewhere inside you, you know I didn't betray you. I'm not in league with Jean Claude." She reached for his hand and curled her fingers around his. "I am who I've always been."

He smiled again, softly, temptingly. "And who is that?"

"Julie," she said with a small smile. "Just Julie."

Noise sounded in the distance. Car doors

slamming, a bus engine rumbling, voices lifting, talking, laughing.

"Our guests are here," he said, straightening up and moving away.

"Travis—" He was pulling back from her and only a moment ago, he'd been so close. So tantalizingly close, she'd thought for a second that he was going to kiss her. To tell her he did trust her. That he believed in her.

. But the moment was gone and the shadows in his eyes smothered the light she'd seen gleaming there so briefly.

The door to the tasting room opened, allowing a slice of afternoon sunlight to spill inside. Voices trailed in the wake of that splash of gold and Julie knew the first of their guests were arriving. "Travis," she said softly, frantically, "I wouldn't betray you."

He only looked at her as though trying to figure out who she really was. But didn't he know? Apparently not.

"By the way," Travis said, his voice carrying subtly beneath the encroaching noise. "You look beautiful tonight."

Staring at her now—her dark red hair, her green eyes wide and innocent, her luscious mouth in a hard firm line—he felt a staggering rush of desire that made him wonder what he was thinking with. His mind or his hormones?

She wore a deep yellow dress with one shoulder strap. The skirt was full and ended just above her knees. He'd seen her dressing only an hour ago and had wanted nothing more than to trail his fingertips down the line of her spine displayed by the deep back of the dress. Now, he still wanted that.

Despite the newspaper photo.

Despite everything…he wanted her.

What did that make him?

A fool?

As the voices behind them grew and came

closer, Travis sucked in a deep breath, held it and then released it slowly, trying to find an even keel again. If only for a short time. Long enough to get through the tasting.

"This isn't the time," he said finally, and told himself not to notice the disappointment in her eyes. She wanted him to give her unconditional trust and belief. But how could he when everything conspired to make him think that she was in league with ol' Pierre?

"Travis—"

"Isn't this *lovely?*" a high-pitched female voice cooed from too close by and Travis shook his head.

"We'll talk about this later," he said quietly. "When we're alone."

Then he folded the newspaper, tucked it under his left arm and turned to face the winery guests. "Welcome to King Vineyards," he called out. "My wife and I hope you enjoy your evening."

Because, he added silently, *somebody* should.

* * *

Over the next several weeks, life settled into a routine of sorts. Julie worked in the kitchen, trying out new recipes, planning for the day when she would have her bakery. Although the excitement of her plans was muted by the fact that once she *had* that bakery, she wouldn't have Travis.

The ache of that thought stayed with her day and night. Every waking moment she wondered how she would spend the rest of her life knowing she wouldn't have him with her. Knowing that she would be sleeping alone, always haunted by the memories of being in his arms. And she wondered if he would miss her, too.

When they hosted the tastings together, she was almost convinced that he thought of them as a team. They worked well together, and over the last few weeks, the King winery had received more visitors than ever. Between

Travis's fine wines and the delicacies Julie made and served, they were the talk of the area.

Now, newspaper articles focused more on the winery itself rather than the scandal that had surrounded them for so long. Julie wasn't sorry to see the end of that disgrace, but she was worried about what Jean Claude might do next. He'd vowed not to stop in his harassment campaign and she had to assume that nothing had changed.

So this respite was probably nothing more than the calm before a new Jean Claude storm.

Not that that was the only thing on her mind. Or even the most *important* thing on her mind. Julie pulled in a deep breath and blew it out again slowly. As a matter of fact, Jean Claude was the last thing on her mind now.

Ever since she'd found the nerve to take a little test.

Stepping away from the cooking island, she turned and walked to the bay window overlooking the vineyard. With Travis's cook on vacation, Julie had the kitchen to herself and right now, she needed the solitude. To think. To decide what to do. What to say.

As it was, Julie felt like an idiot. With everything that had been going on around them, she'd completely forgotten to keep track of her monthly cycle. If she had, she would have noticed sooner that her period hadn't shown up when it should have.

Her gaze fixed on the horizon, she watched as the sinking sun began to paint the clouds deep shades of scarlet and gold. A wind was blowing, ruffling the leaves on the vines and sending a minitornado of dust dancing along the neatly tended rows of grapes.

And inside her, a different kind of tornado was taking shape.

She'd driven to Sacramento that morning,

wanting to get as far from prying eyes and nosy neighbors in Birkfield as possible. She'd bought the pregnancy test kit and smuggled it into the house as if she were a drug dealer. Then the package had sat beneath the bathroom sink all day, taunting her with its presence, silently daring her to take its challenge.

Finally, an hour ago, she had.

It had only taken three short minutes to redefine her life.

One little plus sign and now everything was different.

She felt more alive than she ever had and yet more subdued. Exhilarated and worried.

How could she tell Travis that she was pregnant with his child? This was a temporary marriage. They'd both agreed to that at the beginning.

Besides, even if he wanted her to, she couldn't stay with Travis simply because she was pregnant. If he didn't love her, what would be the point? They'd only end by making each other—and their child—miserable.

"Something wrong?"

Travis's voice jolted Julie out of her thoughts. She slapped one hand to her chest and whirled around to find him standing beside the cook island, watching her. Guilt slipped through her system, but she fought it back down. She was going to tell him so there was no reason for the guilt. "You scared me."

He smiled and snitched one of the tiny lemon tarts she'd taken from the oven only a few minutes ago. Since discovering they were Travis's favorites, she made them often. "Those are still hot."

"I like things hot."

She flushed. Just like that. So easy, he didn't even have to try and she felt a flash of heat inside that would have put her oven to shame. How could she ever spend the rest of her life without him? How could she raise their child without Travis's love in her life?

He blew onto the lemon surface, then took a bite, savoring the tartness. "Delicious. As always."

"Thank you."

"So what were you thinking when I came in?" he asked.

Oh, she couldn't go there. Couldn't even let the thoughts into her mind, because she didn't doubt that somehow, he would *know*. So instead, she thought about how she loved him. About how she wanted to stay with him. Have him love her back. Those thoughts, he would be oblivious to. "Nothing special."

"You're not a very good liar."

"That's a good thing, isn't it?" She forced a smile and swept a dish towel across her left shoulder. Then deftly, she moved the rest of the lemon tarts from the baking tray to a wire rack where they could cool.

"Yeah," Travis admitted. "I guess it is."

Looking at her now, Travis couldn't think of one reason to doubt her. Her hair was pulled back in a ponytail, she wore a dark green King Winery T-shirt and faded blue jeans. Her feet were bare and her toenails were painted a soft peach.

And her eyes met his with a simple honesty that he couldn't force himself to deny.

He kept trying to maintain an emotional distance between them, but that was getting more difficult every day. He was drawn to her. At night, he lost himself in the feel of her, the scent of her, the eagerness she expressed when he touched her.

During the day, he found his mind wandering during meetings. He couldn't walk the vines without thinking of her, wondering what she was doing. And the nights when she stood beside him in the tasting room, he was proud to have her there with him. She was warm and friendly to their guests, making them all feel special, and as word of her talents in the kitchen spread, their tourist traffic had more than doubled. King Winery was making its mark on the state and even Thomas Henry had noticed.

Travis hadn't had to wheedle his way into a distribution deal after all. Henry had come to him with a more than fair offer and there hadn't been any more snide comments about Julie, either.

He took another bite of the lemon tart and savored the delicious mix of sweet and sour that dissolved on his tongue in a burst of flavor.

Sweet and sour. Pretty much described what this temporary marriage of theirs was like. The sweet—those moments when they were together, focused only on each other. The nights in her arms and the laughter in the mornings. The touch of her hand and the sound of her sigh when he joined his body to hers. The knowledge that she was there, in his house when he came in from the vines. It was all so much more than he'd expected to find in a marriage that had been meant to be nothing more than a business deal.

But then there was the sour and that nagged at him. There was the mess with her ex. The way she'd gone behind his back to meet him—even if her reasons had made sense to him. There was the tight feeling in his chest whenever she was out of his sight for too long and the knowledge that in less than a year now, she would be out of his life.

He could hardly imagine her not being a part of his everyday world. Who would he talk to? Who would be there to argue with him over the best way to run a tasting? None of his employees dared to oppose him. But Julie had never had a problem with it. She stood up to him. Stood up for herself. Which is why he could look back at her meeting with Jean

Claude and understand the reasoning behind it. He might not have liked it, but knowing her as he did, he shouldn't have expected anything else.

And on that thought, he said, "I talked to Adam a minute ago. Actually, it was more like me listening, older brother talking."

"About?"

"Pierre, strangely enough."

He saw her flinch just before her gaze dropped to the surface of the cook island.

"What did Adam have to say?"

Travis leaned both hands on the edge of the countertop and felt that straight edge bite into his flesh. He kept his gaze locked on her as he said, "He set a plan into motion. Something that with any luck, will get rid of Jean Claude for good."

She nodded, blew out a breath and finally lifted her gaze to his. "When's this plan supposed to take place?"

"Soon."

"That's good, then."

"Yeah." She didn't look happy, though, and whether he wanted it to or not, a doubt filled whisper scuttled through his mind. *Is she happy to have the Jean Claude situation exposed and ended? Or is she worried that her compliance with him will be uncovered?* Even as that thought whipped through his mind, Travis told himself it just wasn't possible. He didn't want it to be possible.

Irritated, he frowned, straightened up and backed away. She smelled too good, looked too appealing for his own comfort level. "I just wanted to tell you. Keep you up-to-date on what's happening."

"I appreciate it," she said, but she didn't look the slightest bit happy. Instead she looked worried and a little green around the gills.

"Are you feeling all right?" Travis stopped

at the doorway and looked at her closely, noticing for the first time that her skin was paler than usual. That her usually bright eyes looked a little glassy.

"Fine. Just a bit queasy." She gave him a smile that was meant to placate. "Probably tasted too much while I was cooking."

Her answer came fast and easy, but Travis went still and cold. As he'd noted earlier, she was a bad liar.

Ten

"**R**emember our wedding night?"

"Of course I do." Vividly. Travis stared at her, waiting. She looked nervous—the tips of her fingers plucking at the thigh seams on her jeans. She bit down on her bottom lip, shifted her gaze from his, to the wall nearby and then back again. He couldn't recall a single moment in their time together when she'd seemed nervous before. Worried, yes. Scared, pissed off and stubborn, yes. But over the last few weeks, he'd never seen her look shaken.

Until now.

As he watched her, his senses kicked in and he thought maybe he knew exactly why she seemed so on edge all of a sudden.

She opened her mouth, closed it again, then huffed out a breath.

"Just say it, Julie." Travis braced himself for hearing the only words that would explain both her queasiness and the tension that was clearly gripping him.

"I'm pregnant."

He rocked back on his feet as those two simple words punched into his gut. The words he'd somehow expected to hear. In the blink of an eye, everything had changed.

Pregnant.

His gaze dropped to her flat abdomen before lifting to meet her eyes again. She was carrying his child. Even now, that tiny life was growing, already racing toward the finish line of birth.

His baby.

Travis's brain worked frantically. He didn't know what to think. What to feel. How was a man supposed to react when he found out he was going to be someone's *father?*

Panicked, that's how.

That emotion wasn't one Travis had a lot of experience with. He always knew what to do. He never had to wonder if he was making the right decision or not. He was *always* sure of himself. And now, a tiny being the size of his thumbnail had him feeling as if he was sliding off the edge of the earth, scrambling for a handhold to stop his fall.

Scrubbing one hand over his face, Travis told himself he was a man who liked being in charge. A man who made his own choices in life. Now, though, he was a man caught firmly in the grip of a very whimsical Fate.

Travis King…a *father?*

Boggled the mind.

He took a breath and waited a second for it to kick in, maybe air out his mind so his thoughts could clear up. But that obviously wasn't going to happen anytime soon.

"How long have you known?" The words were squeezed out from between clenched teeth. Did it matter when she had found out about the baby? Yes. It did. He had to know if she'd been keeping this from him—the thought of any secrecy irritated him. Or if she would have kept quiet about it altogether had he not asked her flat out what was bothering her.

"An hour," she said and folded her arms around her middle, as if instinctively protecting the child within her body. "I was going to tell you tonight."

An hour. She'd only just found out herself and, judging by the expression on her face, the news was as overwhelming to her as it had been to him. Her eyes looked wide and a little confused. Well, hell. He knew just how she felt.

Travis's chest suddenly tightened to the point where he was half afraid he wouldn't be able to draw another breath. He stared at her as if seeing her for the first time. Her hair shone with dark red and gold lights in the final rays of the dying sun. Her face was pale and her eyes looked huge in her face.

She was more beautiful to him in this moment than he'd ever thought her before. His instincts fired. His woman. His child. Everything in him, everything he'd been taught as a child, his belief system—or morals—railed at him to protect her. To care for her. To stand between her and the world. Hell, it was all he could do to keep from rushing at Julie, lifting her off her feet and carrying her to the nearest chair, forcing her to sit down.

But instead he just stood there, trying to come to grips with the latest wrinkle in his world. He hadn't planned on being a parent. In fact, he'd gone out of his way to insure that he wouldn't be a father. Travis had made it a point in his life to be careful with the women he spent time with. He hadn't wanted to be creating life carelessly with a woman who was no more than a brief blip on his radar.

Now he was married—albeit temporarily—and his wife was pregnant with his baby.

"I know what you're thinking," she said quietly.

"Oh," he said, with a short, sharp burst of laughter. "I doubt that." Hell, even he couldn't keep track of his thoughts. No way she would be able to make sense of them.

"You're wondering if this baby is even yours."

She'd surprised him again.

That thought had never crossed his mind.

Her arms tightened around her middle and she lifted her chin as if trying to win a battle he hadn't even engaged in yet. "It's your baby, Travis. It's *not* Jean Claude's."

He shook his head. "What are you talking about?"

"I know you've had your doubts about me." She paused for a breath. "With the trouble Jean Claude's caused, I can even understand that to a point. But this is different. This is our baby. And I don't want you to think even for a second that—"

"Stop," he said quietly, cutting off her speech because he didn't need to hear it. He hated that she felt as though she had to defend their child to him. Hated that he'd made her feel as if he would doubt her about something this big. "I know it's my baby, Julie. Our baby."

Strange, everything they'd been through the last few weeks, and he hadn't even considered that the child could have been her ex's. Almost laughable now, he thought, that he'd been so incensed by a photo of that Frenchman kissing her. He'd doubted her loyalties. Doubted her feelings.

But on this, he had no doubts.

Julie would never foist another man's child on him. It wasn't in her to be that duplicitous. She was too honest. Too straightforward.

God, he was an idiot.

How could he have ever believed that she was in cahoots with her ex? He should have trusted her. Hadn't he known her long enough to know that she had a core that was as scrupulously honest as his own? Had he really been so thrown by *Pierre's* foolish plans that he was willing to lump Julie in with the man?

It was a wonder she was still speaking to him. Julie simply wasn't the kind of woman to sink to those kinds of games. And he should have realized that simple truth before now.

She blew out a breath and nodded. "Thanks for that."

"You shouldn't be thanking me," he said tightly. "You should be furious at me for not believing in you all along."

She shrugged a little and laid the flat of one hand against her abdomen, as if she were shielding the child within. "I was before," she assured him with a small laugh that sounded strained and tight. "You've made me furious lots of times over the last several weeks, Travis. And sometimes talking to you is like talking to a wall—only the wall would probably listen better."

He winced a little at that, because he recognized it as pure truth. He hadn't been willing to listen. Too intent on his own will, his own way, he hadn't wanted to hear from her unless she'd been agreeing with him.

"But this is…different," she said quietly. "Bigger. The fact that you believe me about this makes up for the rest. Besides, it's been a weird couple of months."

"True." The last couple of months with Julie had seemed like one long roller-coaster ride. Every time he thought they were through the confusion and mess, something new had cropped up. He'd mistrusted her, and wanted her. Suspected her, and desired her.

Now, he realized, the suspicion was gone, leaving only the passion and something else…something warm and deep and… He frowned to himself and shut down that particular train of thought.

"Travis," she said, narrowing her eyes on him. "Are you okay?"

He laughed shortly. He was far from okay. But he wasn't going to admit that to her.

"I honestly don't know." Walking slowly toward her, he said, "This isn't about me, anyway. Are *you* all right?" he asked quietly, giving himself points for holding back the rush of protectiveness that was nearly strangling him.

"I'm fine. A little queasy. A little shocked." She rubbed the flat of her hand across her abdomen and Travis wondered if she was even aware of her actions. "But I'm fine—especially since you're taking this so unexpectedly well."

Didn't make him feel any better that she'd clearly expected him to both doubt her and be upset by this news. Although, now that he thought about it, why *wasn't* he upset by the news of a surprise pregnancy? Yet another thought to avoid.

"You need to see a doctor."

"I was planning to."

"Good." He nodded, his mind already skipping ahead. "I'll want to be there for it."

"Of course."

He inhaled sharply and took in the scent of lemons and vanilla. "I don't want you to worry about anything," he said. "I just want you to take care of yourself. That's the only important thing now."

She smiled as she looked up to meet his gaze. Something inside Travis turned over and tightened. His heart?

He whipped past that thought at breakneck speed. Instead, he started thinking aloud, making plans, working things out in his mind.

"We'll have to set up a nursery, but I don't want you doing any of the work." Nodding to himself, he added, "We'll hire a designer. Architect if you'd rather build a room off of ours instead of using one of the guest rooms. Maybe that would be better. The baby would be closer to us in those first few months. We'd both probably sleep easier that way." It was all coming together for him.

Images drifted into his mind. He and Julie standing alongside their child's crib, looking down at a sleeping infant. Boy? Girl? That thread of panic wormed its way back through him and Travis started speaking again in an effort to squash it. "We could talk to the muralist who did the walls in Gina and Adam's nursery. She did a whole magical kingdom kind of thing in there and it looks pretty great—"

"Travis…"

"And I don't want you doing the cooking for the tastings anymore," he blurted. Taking her arm, he steered her toward one of the chairs at the small, round breakfast table at the far end of the kitchen. "You shouldn't be on your feet so much."

"Travis, I don't want to sit down," she said.

He hardly heard her as he gently shoved her down onto a chair. "When our cook gets back from her vacation, you can go over the menus with her. I'm sure Margaret can handle what you've been doing for the winery—"

"*Travis!*"

"What?"

She stood up to face him and he only just managed to refrain from pushing her back down onto the chair. "What're you doing?" she asked.

Baffled, he said, "Making plans."

"I can see that." She shook her head. "The question is, *why?*"

"Why? Because we're going to have a baby. We need to start thinking about these things."

"No, we don't."

Something cold and hard settled in his chest, making him feel as if a boulder had been rolled onto his rib cage. "What're you saying? You don't want the baby?"

She jerked back and stared at him as if he'd suggested she pop her head off her shoulders and set it onto the counter. "Of *course* I want the baby. How could you even think—"

"Then what's this about?"

"Travis, we don't have a real marriage. Remember?" Her voice was soft, but her words slapped at him. "This was a temporary business deal. We're only going to be together for a year."

That had been the deal.

But things had changed.

As if she heard him, she said, "The baby doesn't change that. We're not your usual expectant couple. I know we didn't plan on this," she said, her eyes shining up at him. "But I want you to know that even after our year together is up, you'll always have access to your child. I would never keep it from you."

Travis scowled as her words sunk in and rattled around his mind. Did she really think he'd let her go now? Didn't she know that their "bargain" had just changed? There was no "temporary" to this marriage anymore.

Access? To his child? Visits on weekends? Oh, no. That wasn't going to happen.

He dropped both hands onto her shoulders and held on tightly. Looking deeply into her eyes, he said, "You're wrong, Julie. Our marriage just became permanent. Think 'until death us do part.' We won't be splitting up in a year."

"But—"

"Do you really think I'd let you go now? You're having my baby, Julie."

"It will still be your baby after we're divorced."

"Not going to happen."

"Travis, I can't stay married simply because of our child. It wouldn't be right. Or good. For any of us."

"Divorce would be better?" His voice was steel. As was his resolve. There would be no divorce. Julie wouldn't be leaving him and taking his child. They could work this out together. Find a way to be happy. The three of them.

"Travis…"

"We're having a baby and we're staying married," he said, pulling her into his arms, ignoring the fact that she moved stiffly. "Get used to it."

"He won't listen." Julie sat at the kitchen table of the King ranch and watched as a hugely pregnant Gina King moved slowly across the room.

"Big surprise there," Gina muttered, reaching down four glasses from a cabinet over the kitchen counter and setting them on a tray beside a pitcher of iced tea. She shot a look at Julie. "Dealing with the King men can be cause for buying the economy-size bottle of aspirin."

Get used to it.

Travis's words echoed over and over again in her mind, as they'd been doing for the last few days. But how could she do that, Julie wondered. How could she ever settle for a marriage that was maintained simply for the sake of her child?

How could she ever live with Travis knowing she loved him but that he would never return the feelings?

"I can't do it," she whispered. "I just can't."

"It's hard," Gina said softly. "Being the one in love."

Julie's gaze snapped to her sister in law. "You, too?"

The overhead lights in the kitchen shone down on the other woman, illuminating her so brightly, she almost seemed to glow. She looked so content, so completely happy and at home, Julie felt a quick stab of envy.

Gina rubbed one hand over the mound of her child and smiled to herself. "I've loved Adam all my life. I always thought it would be one of those tragic unrequited love stories." Her smile blossomed into a grin. "But you know what? Sometimes the men we love can surprise us. Sometimes, they wake up and see what's staring them in the face."

"Sometimes," Julie admonished with shake of her head. "But Travis is much more stubborn than Adam or Jackson. He's got a head like solid cement, I swear."

"Just don't give up on him too soon," Gina told her, lifting a jug of tea to pour into the glasses. "Oh."

Julie leaped up from her chair, hurried

across the kitchen and took Gina's arm. "Are you okay? You shouldn't be on your feet like this. Let me do it, for heaven's sake." She stopped, sighed and said, "I sound like Travis talking to me."

"You think he's bad now?" Gina asked. "Wait until the baby's three days overdue. Adam practically carries me to the bathroom every morning."

"He loves you."

"He really does." Gina looked into Julie's eyes and said softly, "And here's something to think about. If Travis is that worried about you, don't you think he might love you, too?"

Julie threw a glance at the door separating the kitchen from the dining room and the rest of the house beyond. God help her, she'd like to believe that Travis loved her. But even if he claimed to now, how would she ever know if he meant it—or if because of the baby, he was only saying the words she needed to hear?

"Come on. Let's get you into the study," Julie said, putting her own worries and fears aside for the moment. "I'll carry the tray."

"You know what? I think I'll let you."

In the study, there was a fire in the hearth. Soft lighting from lamps scattered around the room added to the coziness created by the dancing shadows of the flames. The three King brothers were seated in the wide, maroon leather chairs and all three of them leaped to their feet when the women entered the room.

"You shouldn't be carrying heavy things," Travis said as he scooped the serving tray out of Julie's hands.

"It's not heavy," she argued, but had already lost the battle.

"You okay, honey?" Adam was asking as he steered Gina to a chair and lowered her down onto it with all the care of a man handling a live explosive.

"I'm fine," she said. "I'm just feeling a little tired and achy."

"Achy?" Adam's voice went up a notch. "You're in pain? Have you timed them? When did it start?"

"Not that kind of pain." Gina laughed and patted his hand. "It's just a backache."

"Are you sure—"

"Geez, Adam," Jackson said from across the room. "Let her get some air. If she's in labor, she'll tell us."

Adam shot him a look that should have fried him on the spot, but Jackson only laughed and took a sip of his Irish whiskey.

Travis frowned at his younger brother. Jackson just didn't get it. The worry. The fear. Ever since finding out that Julie was pregnant, he hadn't been able to think of anything else. And rather than laugh at his older brother's barely restrained panic, Travis completely sympathized. One part of him was terrified of what he would face in another eight months…and another part of him couldn't wait.

It was like being a split personality, he thought. He could literally stand back and watch himself be an ass. He kept a close watch on Julie at all times and worried like hell when she was out of his sight. He didn't know how he was going to make it through the pregnancy intact.

And beside the general worries was one he was sure Adam hadn't had to contend with. The concern that his wife would pack up and move out at the end of their year together. Not that she'd get far. Travis would follow and bring her back where she belonged, of course. But at the same time, he didn't want her to *want* to leave. He wanted her as committed as he now was to building their family.

He frowned, then told himself that he still had plenty of time to make her see things his way. For now, he would simply take care of her. And as Jackson chuckled again, Travis sincerely hoped that one day, the youngest King brother got a hard dose of reality all for himself, and then they'd see who was doing the laughing.

Travis got Julie into a chair, then poured iced tea for everyone but Jackson. When they were all settled, he looked to Adam. "Well? Everyone's gathered. Let's do this."

"What's going on?" Julie asked.

"You're about to find out," Travis said.

Looking very pleased with himself, Adam walked to his massive desk on the far side of the room. He grabbed a tape recorder off the surface and walked back to the group. Looking from one to the other of them, Adam started with an explanation for the ladies.

"Obviously, you two know that Travis, Jackson and I hired a P.I. to look into Jean

Claude's background." The women nodded. "As you also know, we didn't find anything that could be seen as illegal in the strictest sense."

Julie shifted uneasily, but Travis dropped one hand onto her shoulder and gave it a squeeze. "Quit telling them what they already know and get on to the rest of it, Adam," he said, wanting Julie's discomfort over as fast as possible.

"Right." The oldest King brother smiled at them all and said, "The P.I. had another idea that we all agreed was worth a try. We didn't say anything to you two—" he nodded at Julie and Gina "—because we didn't want to get your hopes up for a resolution if this idea failed. But it didn't."

"What did you do?" Julie turned her face up to Travis and he smiled down at her. It hadn't been easy not telling her this news. He'd known about it all day, but he and Adam had decided to spring it on everyone at once.

Which was why the family meeting had been called so suddenly.

"Our P.I. hired a woman to cozy up to Pierre," Travis said, a tight, victorious smile curving his lips. "She was supposed to flirt, come on to him and get him drunk enough to spill his guts. I didn't really believe your ex would be stupid enough to fall for it. But turns out, he's not the freshest croissant in the bakery."

Jackson snorted.

Adam bent down, and set the tape recorder on the coffee table. "It lasts for quite a while," he said. "The poor woman sat with this jerk for over an hour, plying him with expensive booze until she hit pay dirt. I've cued the tape to the part we wanted you two to hear." Then he hit the play button.

"And her husband is going to pay you?" A throaty, female voice rolled out from the tape recorder.

"Oh, he will pay me whatever I ask." Jean

Claude's voice came next. The words were slurred, but perfectly audible. *"He believes my lies about his little Julie. And he will continue to pay as long as I can keep him believing that she still loves only me."*

Beneath his hand, Travis felt Julie stiffen slightly and he squeezed her shoulder again in solidarity. He knew how hard it must be for her to listen to this, because he wanted nothing more than to hunt Jean Claude down and beat the crap out of him for all the trouble he'd caused.

"But isn't blackmail dangerous?"

"And very lu-lur-lucrative," Jean Claude said on a hiccup. *"I will tell him Julie meets me for sex and he will pay me again. And again."*

Travis scowled at the tape recorder as Julie gasped and said hotly, "He's lying."

"Of course he's lying," Adam sneered. He bent to shut off the tape. "That's enough.

None of us should have to listen to more of that idiot. But believe me when I say the police were *very* interested in this tape. Soon, Jean Claude's going to be too busy covering his own ass to cause us any more problems."

"But once the police have this evidence, it'll go to court and all of this will be back in the news," Julie said softly, covering her flat belly with her hand as if trying to keep the baby from hearing any of this.

"No." Travis waited until she looked up at him before he said, "I'm going to offer Jean Claude his last deal. If he leaves the country and keeps his mouth shut, I won't press charges."

"What about the money you already paid him?"

"Doesn't matter," he said.

"So it's over?" Julie asked.

"Over," Travis said. "He won't bother you again, Julie. I swear it."

She smiled. "And your contract for your wines?"

"Sewn up," Travis said. "Struck a deal this afternoon."

"Well this is good news!" Jackson lifted his glass in salute. "Finally, the Kings can relax a little."

"Not so fast," Gina muttered, as her water broke.

Eleven

Her name was Emma.

Eight pounds five ounces of beautiful baby girl.

Gina King's hospital room was lavishly appointed and filled with so many flowers, it looked like an English garden. The air was scented with perfume and rocked with laughter and eager conversations. After eight hours of labor, Gina herself looked exhausted but exhilarated. And as she held court over the family that crowded in close to get a look at the baby, the new mother practically radiated joy.

"She's a beauty, Adam," Travis said with a grin. "Lucky for her, she looks just like her mother."

"I couldn't agree more," Adam said and bent down to kiss his wife's forehead.

Julie's eyes were blurry with tears as she watched Gina's parents, the Torinos, coo over their latest grandchild. Standing right beside them was Adam, who only managed to tear his gaze from his wife long enough to stare wide-eyed at his daughter. Jackson and Travis were both there, each of them delighted by their new niece. Julie had had a turn at holding the newborn and as she cradled that tiny scrap of life, she'd suddenly felt both a part of the crowd, and somehow distant from them all, too. When she handed Emma back to her doting father, Julie stepped back, so that she could see them all, watch the scene with an objective eye.

She didn't begrudge Gina and Adam their joy, but as she watched her brother-in-law smiling tenderly at his family, she couldn't help but wish that Travis would feel the same way toward her and the child they'd created together.

But she wasn't foolish enough to try to lie to herself about it, either. Travis was doing what he considered the right thing. Julie knew he would make a life with her whether he'd wanted one or not. He would welcome their child and love it, but he would never love *her.*

And how could she stay with a man who only remained married to her because of his own sense of duty?

The answer was simple.

She couldn't.

New tears filled her eyes, but she blinked them back. This moment wasn't about her. Or Travis. This moment, this time, was for Gina and Adam and their daughter. There would be time enough later to talk to Travis. To tell him that no matter what he did, she wouldn't be staying with him at the end of their year together.

But that decision was followed quickly by a horrible thought. What if he decided to fight her for custody of their child? What then? That thought gave Julie a cold chill that snaked along her spine and made her shiver. She wouldn't have the resources to fight him in court. So whether she wanted to stay or not, did she really have a choice?

Must she just somehow accustom herself to the idea of living a half life—loving a man and knowing that he would never return that love? She'd trapped herself in a velvet box.

A cage with no bars.

She didn't want to stay, but couldn't leave.

"Are you all right?" Travis was there suddenly, right beside her. His voice was deep and soft, so that only she could hear him. He touched her face, fingertips light on her cheek and the buzz of heat shot through her at the connection, firing up her blood, easing the ice around her heart.

"I'm fine," she lied. "Just tired, I guess."

His eyes were worried, but he smiled at her just the same. "Not surprising. And now that the show's over, I'll take you home. You should be getting some rest anyway."

She loved the way he wanted to take care of her. She only wished it was because he loved her.

"Probably a good idea," she said, suddenly so fatigued she didn't know if she could stay upright another ten minutes.

They said their goodbyes and left the private room to walk along the hospital corridor. In the middle of the night, the lights in the hallways seemed harsh. A baby wailed in the distance and two nurses huddled behind a counter, looking over a chart. Machines beeped, families paced the corridors and the sounds of their shoes clicked loudly against the linoleum.

Travis took Julie's hand in his and tried to find his equilibrium again. He'd lost it sometime during the long night they'd just passed. Watching Adam, usually a rock of emotional calm, turn into a harried, frantic man standing on the edge of panic had warned Travis of exactly what awaited him in just a few short months. He'd felt Adam's nerves, experienced the fear right along with him and then the amazing joy that had followed all the terror.

And staring down into the face of that tiny, beautiful baby girl, Travis had felt something else. Something he hadn't expected to hit him so hard. Something he was still dealing with.

Love.

Rich and full and complicated. The baby had been alive less than an hour and already, it was as if she'd always been here. She was a King. His brother's daughter. Travis knew that if it came to it, he would lay down his own life for that child.

So, he had to wonder, how much bigger would the feelings be for his own baby? He couldn't even imagine emotions that huge.

"Quite a night," he said as he stabbed the elevator button.

Julie nodded. "Gina was amazing."

"She was." Travis tucked a strand of dark red hair behind Julie's ear and indulged himself by then cupping her cheek in his palm. "You are, too."

She laughed shortly. "I haven't done anything yet."

He shook his head and laid one hand against her belly. "Haven't you? You're *making* a child, Julie."

"Travis," she said as the elevator dinged and the doors swished open. "Are you okay?"

He wasn't sure. He only knew that as he

looked down into those green eyes that had haunted him from their very first night together, that he was feeling something different. Something…

"Yeah. I'm fine." He took her elbow and steered her into the elevator for the short ride from the second floor to the first. He pushed the down button, the doors closed and a moment later, the world dropped out from beneath their feet.

Julie's scream seemed to echo forever.

Only seconds later, though it felt like hours, Travis picked himself up off the elevator floor and crawled to where Julie lay sprawled in a corner. The elevator hadn't dropped all that far. Just the one floor. But the jolting crash had sounded like a sonic boom and had clearly stunned her.

Dust drifted down from the ceiling and the elevator light flickered wildly.

Travis's head hurt, his body ached and nothing was more important to him than reaching Julie. Her eyes fluttered open when he called her name.

"What happened?"

"I don't know," he muttered, running his hands up and down her body, checking for breaks, for bruises. "Are you hurt? Can you move?"

"Everything hurts," she said, her voice catching in a way that tore at Travis's chest. "But I think I can move."

He held her as she shifted to sit upright, back braced against the wall. She lifted one hand to her forehead and a jolt of pure fear ripped through him when he saw a tiny rivulet of blood rolling along her skin.

"You're bleeding," he muttered and quickly patted his pockets for something to stop it with, even knowing he didn't usually carry a handkerchief tucked into his jeans pockets.

"Oh, boy," she whispered and rested her head against the wall. "My ears are ringing, too."

"That's the alarm," he said, glancing up and over his shoulder as if he could see the source of the sound and shut it down with the force of his will alone.

"That's good." She laughed a little, hissed in a breath and then gasped.

"What?" he demanded. "What is it? What's wrong?"

She lifted her gaze to his and in the flickering of the overhead light, shadows filled her green eyes and glistened in the sheen of unshed tears. Grabbing his hand, she held on tight and whispered, "I think something's wrong. With the baby."

The overhead light flickered again and went out, plunging them into blackness.

Hours later, Julie hurt all over.

It turned out that the elevator cable was

frayed and had given way. Thankfully, they'd only fallen one floor. If they'd been on the fourth floor when the elevator had dropped, things might have been different for them. As it was, Travis had a few bruises but was mostly unscathed by the accident. Julie was still waiting to find out exactly how badly she'd been injured.

But the aches and pains in her legs and arms didn't worry Julie. The only thing bothering her now was the cramping that had her praying frantically for the safety of her child. It had taken what felt like forever for the Birkfield fire department to arrive and extricate them from the elevator car. Through it all, Travis had been there, holding her, talking to her, trying to ease her fears while they sat huddled in the dark together.

When they were finally free, Julie had been whisked off to be examined. The doctors had run tests and taken blood and now had her hooked up to an IV that made her feel as though fear was filling her, one drip at a time.

Why did she need the IV? Was the baby still with her? Had it already given up its tenuous hold on life and was even now sliding free of her body?

Tears filled her throat, choking her, making each breath a victory. Dread and worry were her constant companions. She'd been so happy earlier, enjoying the celebration of new life with the rest of the King family. Now, everything was different.

Here in her lovely, private hospital room on the medical floor, there were no babies' cries to comfort her. Only the silence of night broken occasionally by the conversations of nurses. Travis had gone—at her insistence—to tell Adam and Gina what was happening, leaving Julie alone, trapped in her bed, waiting to hear if her child would live or die.

And if she lost the baby? Grief welled up

inside her. Misery both for the loss of a child she dearly wanted and the loss of Travis.

Over the last few days, since he'd found out about the baby, Travis had been amazing. He'd made her love him even more and though she'd like to pretend that his actions were prompted by his love for her, Julie knew better.

He was solicitous. Kind. Concerned.

Overbearing.

Dictatorial.

But…he didn't love her. He was only doing what he thought was right. Taking charge of the woman who was carrying his child.

And with the loss of their baby, all of that would end as well. He wouldn't want to continue their marriage once the reason for it was gone. So she would lose everything. Gently, she lay both hands on her belly, as if she could keep her child safe, convince it to stay with her.

For all their sakes.

A standing lamp in the corner threw out a puddle of soft gold light that reached for her from the shadows. The machine on her right beeped and clicked and measured each of her heartbeats.

And still she waited.

When the door to her room opened, she expected to find a dour-faced doctor standing there. Instead, it was Travis. Backlit from the hallways, she couldn't see his features, but every line of his body was tense. He walked to her side quickly, took a seat beside her bed and gathered up one of her hands in his.

"How are Adam and Gina?"

"Worried about you," he said.

"They shouldn't be," she told him, shifting her gaze to the dimly lit ceiling above. "This is a night they should be celebrating."

"We'll celebrate together after we hear from the damn doctor," Travis assured her.

Celebrate what? she wondered. The loss of

everything that mattered? Would he be relieved? Sad? Was he feeling what she was at all?

"You haven't seen the doctor again yet?"

"No," she said with a careful shake of her head, that still caused an eruption of a headache.

He fired a dark look at the closed door. "What's taking them so long? How hard is it to look at ultrasounds? Why can't they just tell us?"

"They can't tell us. The doctor has to. So we have to wait."

Turning back to her, he reached across, touched the bandage on her forehead and asked, "Are you in pain?"

A single tear spilled over and rolled down her cheek. Pain? She was in so much pain it was a wonder she could draw breath. But the small cut on her forehead had nothing to do with this pain. This particular agony went soul deep. "I'm fine."

"Of course you are," he said tightly, giving

her a nod that said she was definitely all right and he wouldn't accept anything less. "Everything's going to be good, Julie. You'll see."

"Travis…" She wanted to tell him she understood that he was only there because it was the right thing to do. That he didn't really want the baby that she was desperately trying to keep. That she didn't expect him to stay there with her. To not make promises he couldn't keep.

But she couldn't make herself say the words to let him go. For as long as she had him, she wanted Travis with her. When he brushed a kiss across her knuckles, she savored the contact, holding it close.

The door opened again and this time, the doctor stepped inside. Instinctively, she grabbed at Travis's hand and held on tight. The doctor walked to the end of Julie's bed, glanced at the chart in his hand then looked up at her and smiled. "Your baby's fine, Mrs. King."

Julie released a breath she hadn't even realized she'd been holding. Relief and gratitude swept through her in such an amazing rush of sensation, she was nearly blinded by her own tears. She had to blink them away to see the doctor clearly. "You're sure?"

"Absolutely. That's a tough kid you've got there," the doctor told her. "Stubborn and determined to be born."

"Naturally he's stubborn," Travis said, grinning like a loon. "He's a King."

"He or she is definitely healthy, so I don't want you worried," the doctor said, gazing meaningfully at Julie. He glanced at her chart again as if reassuring himself. "Doctor's orders."

"Thank you." She was still holding on to Travis's hand, still drawing strength from him, still relishing the touch of his hand on hers.

"Yes," Travis added. "Thank you. But what

about my wife? How is Julie? Is she going to be all right?"

"Your wife is fine, Mr. King." The doctor tucked her chart under his left arm and smiled benevolently. "A little bruised, a little battered and I'll want her to take it easy for a couple of weeks…but she's going to be fine."

Travis dropped Julie's hand, jumped up, pumped the doctor's hand like a wildman and said, "Thank you. I'll see to it that she rests."

Julie watched him as Travis walked the doctor to the door. When it was closed and they were alone again, Julie realized that she'd never known a person could be both happy *and* sad at the same time. She was grateful for the safety of her baby, but now she knew she would remain trapped in a marriage with a man who didn't love her.

Her heart broke a little as she imagined the long empty years ahead of them. And she wondered how long it would be before her soul, denied love, began to die a little each day.

Travis came to her side and gently eased himself down onto the edge of the bed. He smoothed her tangled hair back from her face and leaned down to tenderly touch her lips with his. When he sat back again, he looked into her eyes and said softly, "I've never been so scared in my life. Hell, I didn't know it was *possible* to be that scared."

Touched, Julie patted his hand. "I know you were worried, Travis. So was I. But thank heaven, the baby's fine. You heard the doctor."

"I'm not talking about the baby."

She blinked up at him as if trying to understand. "But—"

"It's *you* Julie. *You* I was terrified for." He took a breath, blew it out and stood up abruptly as if he knew he was too tense to sit quietly on the edge of her bed. Stalking off a

few steps, he whirled around to look at her, sil-
houetted by the golden lamplight. "Do you
know what it was like to feel that damned
elevator fall? To hear you scream? To look
across the floor of the car and see you laying
there in obvious pain? To be *helpless?*"

Before she could speak, he held one hand up
for her silence, then stabbed that hand through
his hair. Shaking his head, he said, "Of course
you don't. I never thought I could feel so
much. Fear so much. Always in my life, I've
charted my own course. Been in charge of my
own destiny. Things happen when I want them
to happen."

"Travis—"

He stared into her eyes as if willing her to
believe every word he said. "Suddenly, there
was nothing I could do. Everything was taken
out of my hands. You were hurt and I couldn't
help you. I could hardly breathe until I
touched you. Couldn't think until you opened

your eyes and looked at me. Couldn't live until I knew *you* were alive."

A bubble of hope began to swell in Julie's chest, warming her through, filling her with the kind of wonder a child found on Christmas morning.

"My own heart stopped, Julie," he said, his words coming fast and furious in a deep whisper that shook her to her core because they were so obviously torn from his soul. He slapped one hand to his chest. "I felt it. The world stopped until you looked at me. Until I could wrap my arms around you and feel your warmth."

Tears were flowing freely now and Julie didn't even make an attempt to stop them.

He walked back to her, and when he was close enough, she could see what she'd long dreamed of seeing in his eyes.

Love. And she hardly dared to believe it.

"I love our baby, don't get me wrong," he said, making sure she understood exactly what he was saying. "And I'm more grateful than I can say that it's healthy and safe." He laid one hand atop hers, and together they cradled the child they'd made. "But without *you*, there's nothing. I need you to know this, Julie. I need you to believe me on this. I *love* you. More than I thought it was possible to love anyone."

"Oh, Travis…"

"I can't lose you. I won't lose you." He bent down, kissed her once, twice. Then he pulled his head back to look into her eyes again. "You're everything to me, Julie. I don't know when it happened, but somehow, during the last couple of months, you've become the center of my world. Without you, there's nothing. Without you, *I'm* nothing."

Smiling through her tears, Julie lifted one hand to cover his cheek. He turned his face into her hand and laid one kiss on the center of her palm. Julie's heart melted and the last of her doubts slid away.

She had everything she'd ever wanted. More than she'd ever really hoped for. Her baby was safe and so was her heart. She looked into his dark brown eyes and saw their future, a bright and shining thing, stretching out in front of them. And she could hardly wait to get out of the hospital and start living it.

"I love you so much," Travis said, capturing her hand and holding it in his. "Tell me you love me, too, or I'm going to go crazy. You have to love me, Julie."

"I do. I do love you, Travis. So very much. I think I always have."

"Thank God," he said, smiling, bending to kiss her again, as if he couldn't get enough of her. "And I'm going to personally see to it that you never change your mind."

* * * * *